Kathy Lyons

IN GOOD HANDS

TORONTO NEW YORK LONDON
AMSTERDAM PARIS SYDNEY HAMBURG
STOCKHOLM ATHENS TOKYO MILAN MADRID
PRAGUE WARSAW BUDAPEST AUCKLAND

Recycling programs
for this product may
not exist in your area.

ISBN-13: 978-0-373-79603-8

IN GOOD HANDS

Printed in U.S.A.

ABOUT THE AUTHOR

Kathy Lyons writes light, funny, sexy stories for the Harlequin Blaze line. She loves the faster pace of category books and that she can really let her humor fly. She leaves the dark, tortured love stories to her alter ego, Jade Lee. A *USA TODAY* bestseller, Jade writes sizzling romances in sexy, dark historical settings. In her spare time, Kathy loves kicking butt on a racquetball court and is a state champion. Jade, on the other hand, loves kicking back and watching the Syfy channel with her husband. Visit them both on the web at www.kathylyons.com or www.jadeleeauthor.com!

Books by Kathy Lyons

HARLEQUIN BLAZE
535—UNDER HIS SPELL
576—TAKING CARE OF BUSINESS

Don't miss any of our special offers. Write to us at the following address for information on our newest releases.

Harlequin Reader Service
U.S.: 3010 Walden Ave., P.O. Box 1325, Buffalo, NY 14269
Canadian: P.O. Box 609, Fort Erie, Ont. L2A 5X3

1

DR. AMBER SMITHSON leaned across the table, nearly dunking her silk blouse into her salad dressing. "Well?" she whispered to the goth-dressed teen across from her. "What'd he say?"

Lizzy did a quick scan of the room, looking quite dramatic in her dark eye liner and studded dog collar.

"Don't worry," said Amber. "I already checked. No one from the hospital is here." Then she patted the table. "Come on, give. What'd he say?"

Lizzy took a deep breath, and for a moment Amber feared the worst. And then the girl burst into a big smile. "My blood test came back *amazing!* That's what he said. Amazing! He doesn't quite believe it."

"Of course he doesn't." Dr. Bob Brickers was as traditional a doctor as they came. He still thought penicillin was cutting edge. He would never accept that a special tea plus some energy sessions done by Amber could possibly bring type 1 diabetes under control. "So everything looks good?" Amber pressed, a little shocked herself that it was working.

"I'm producing insulin on my own! That's what he said. Pretty soon I'll be able to get off the shots completely!"

Amber held up her hands. "One step at a time. The diabetes is under control. That's huge. But—"

"I know! I know! And I didn't say a word to Dr. Brickers about what we're doing. But I know it will work!"

Amber smiled, her own hopes rising. As a doctor at Mandolin Clinic, Amber couldn't possibly admit she was prescribing holistic treatments to anyone, least of all Dr. Brickers's patients. After all, the man was Amber's direct boss. But Lizzy's mom was a friend and had begged Amber for help when the normal treatments had little effect. So Amber had prescribed a special tea and done energy work on the kid. And it was working!

"Just keep doing what you're doing—especially the diet and exercise."

"I know, I know," Lizzy said with a very dramatic eye roll. "And I won't tell anyone or you'll get fired. But it's working!"

Yes, it certainly looked like it was. The two spent the rest of the lunch hour giggling like little girls, then Amber dropped Lizzy back at school before returning to the hospital.

Some days it was hard keeping her interest in holistic healing secret from the ultra-conservative administration at Mandolin. But days like today made it all worth it. That was the reason she'd become a doctor: to find out what worked and what didn't, no matter the source. Her colleagues might think she was nuts, but she didn't care if it was Eastern, Western or alien medicine. If it worked, then she was going to embrace it even if it dealt with something as loosy-goosy as "qi energy."

If only she could get her colleagues to be so open-minded. Some of them were, but the administration was firmly entrenched in the "Western medicine is God" mode, especially Dr. Brickers and his cronies. And until they left or retired, nothing would change at Mandolin.

She lived for that day, prayed nightly for it. Because frankly, she was running out of patience. She'd picked this hospital because it was expected of her. Six generations of Smithsons had worked here as orderlies, then nurses, and then her grandfather had become a doctor here. Her mother, too. So she'd caved to family pressure because Mandolin really was a good hospital and a prestigious place to work.

Then she'd discovered how very narrow-minded her boss was. Not only was alternative medicine evil, in his mind, but anyone who explored it was the devil's handmaiden. No doctor under his watch could suggest anything but traditional Western medicine. So Amber had hidden her interest. She saw patients like Lizzy on her lunch hour, off of hospital grounds. But she was getting tired all the subterfuge.

She was still absorbed in those gloomy thoughts when she stepped through the door and was ambushed by Dr. Jack Ross, her best friend and an extremely talented neurologist. He matched steps with her and was obviously bursting with news.

"Guess who's just killed his last patient," he said as they stepped into the empty elevator.

"Oh, God," she gasped. "Not another!" They were in a hospital, and people died in hospitals. But lately, the mortality rate at Mandolin was unusually high. It happened sometimes, but it never failed to raise alarms among the people in charge. Who then went crusading around desperately looking for an answer. Or a scapegoat.

"Yup. But this time the family's lodged a complaint and it's been backed up by a fellow doctor."

The elevator doors open, and before Amber could move to her office, Jack gripped her arm and steered her to a doctor's lounge. It was thankfully empty at the moment, but that wouldn't last. Before long, practically the whole staff would wander through looking for more gossip to dish. Amber asked the first question on her mind.

"Who died?" Was it someone she knew?

Jack shrugged. "Some woman. Mother of four. Eldest is a lawyer and making all sorts of noise."

"A name, please."

He responded with the diagnosis. "Uterine cancer but she died of a heart attack. Why aren't you asking *whose* patient she was?"

Because she knew. There was only one doctor that Jack desperately wanted gone. The same doctor who was a pain in Amber's backside. Dr. Bob Brickers.

"Keep your voice down," she whispered as she leaned forward. "What happened? Exactly."

"Remember how Bob took that long vacation last month? Well, he pushed up this woman's radiation treatment before she was ready. He wanted to get things going before he left. Anyway, she was too weak to do radiation, so *bam,* last night she has a heart attack and dies."

Amber felt her mouth go slack. Bob couldn't be that irresponsible. Sure, everyone jostled their schedules when they wanted to take a vacation, but to endanger a patient like that? Especially one who...

Her eyes widened and her breath got short. "Wait a moment," she breathed. "Who was the patient? What was her name?"

Jack straightened, alarm growing on his face as he realized something was up. "I don't remember. Vera someone, I think."

"Vera Barker?"

"I don't know."

But Amber did. It all made sense in the most horrible way. She closed her eyes, fighting the tears. To think that Vera was gone. That she would never trade vegetarian recipes with her again. That no one would ever hear her weird horsey laugh again. That her grandchildren would never know how absolutely special she was. The very idea made her heart break. "Not Vera," she whispered. "Oh, God, not Vera."

Two hours later, she was having the exact same discussion in the director's office. Dr. Brickers was there, his face hot and his expression furious. And he was pointing a finger at her.

"Did you or did you not see my patient behind my back?" demanded Dr. Brickers.

Amber sighed and addressed her words to the director. "Vera came to me. She was incredibly weak from the chemotherapy and she had heard about some herbal teas."

"You did!" Brickers all but screamed. "You gave her some holistic crap behind my back, and now she's dead."

Amber didn't bother looking at her boss. Instead, she spoke as calmly and clearly as possible. "My treatments were working, sir. She was getting stronger. But she wasn't ready for radiation yet. Dr. Brickers pushed up her radiation just so he could go on vacation."

"That's not true!" bellowed her boss. But he shut his mouth when the director held up his hand.

"That's not relevant, Amber," said the head of the hospital. "Did you or did you not see Dr. Brickers's patient?"

Amber sighed but stayed with the truth. "I did."

"And you prescribed some herbal tea?"

"And certain energy treatments, yes. And they were working!"

The director just shook his head. "You know that's against hospital policy. You can't see someone else's patient behind his back. You can't prescribe non-traditional treatments. My God, Amber, what were you thinking?"

Amber threw up her hands. "That it was *working!*"

"Except that she's dead," inserted Dr. Brickers.

"Because you pushed up her radiation before she was ready."

The director sighed. "You can't have it both ways, Amber. Either she was stronger or she wasn't."

"Sir!"

"I'm afraid my hands are tied, Amber. You broke hospital policy, you deliberately went behind your boss's back and now a patient is dead."

Amber took a deep breath, struggling to keep her temper in check. "You're right, sir. I should have told Dr. Brickers that Vera contacted me. I'm sorry and it will never happen again. But you can't blame the treatment for—"

The director held up his hand. "Who administered this so-called energy treatment?"

"I did, sir. It's very safe. It works with the body's qi energy—"

"Is it approved by the American Medical Association as an appropriate treatment for cancer?"

Amber grimaced. "You know it's not."

"Then I'll have to ask for your resignation."

Amber's eyes widened in shock even though she'd known this was a possibility. "You're firing me? Even if the treatment worked? Even if the patient got stronger and healthier because of it?"

The director just shook his head. "We can't have doctors practicing non-traditional medicine here at Mandolin. It's just not the way we do things."

"Even if it works?"

"Even if. The liability is too high." Then he leaned forward, his expression almost pleading. "Look, I know we're all under a lot of pressure. We're a high-profile hospital and our patients *must* get better."

"That's what I was trying to do," she said.

"But not the right way, Amber. Still, if you'll promise to stop with all this qi nonsense then I'll soften this to an official reprimand. You're a great doctor, Amber. It would be a shame to lose you."

"The qi nonsense works, sir. I've done a lot of research on my own, but real statistics would be incredibly valuable. Let me do a study—"

Beside her, Dr. Brickers snorted his derision. "Oh, my God, how can you be so idiotic?"

The director also wasn't swayed. "Stick to Western medicine, Amber, and don't talk about Eastern voodoo."

There it was plain as day. If she wanted to work as a doctor, she had to close her eyes to energy healing. She had to pretend that drugs were the only way to treat an illness. That nothing outside of traditional Western medicine had any value at all. She couldn't do that. She just couldn't.

"I can't willingly put blinders on. I'm a healer, sir. From the core of my being, I work to heal people. So if a treatment works, I'll prescribe it."

"Western medicine works," the director said.

"Not for everybody." With a heavy heart, she turned and headed for the door. "You'll have my resignation in an hour."

2

Two years later

ROGER MARTELL stared at his doctor and tried reaching for humor. "That's it? That's why you dragged me in here? Geez, I thought I was dying!"

His doctor sighed. "Hypertension *is* a big deal. And if you don't get it under control you *will* die."

Roger flinched, a little frightened by the man's flat, absolute tone. Sadly, he wasn't surprised by the diagnosis. After all, he'd been fighting high blood pressure forever. His uncle and grandfather had both died from heart attacks before their fiftieth birthdays. And Roger was well on the early coronary track. But advances in medicine happened every day, right? He wasn't desperate yet.

"Okay," he said. "So this special new drug trial didn't work."

"Your pressure is higher than ever, Roger."

"I know, I know," he groused. This was his first drug trial, but his thirteenth medication. No matter what he did, his blood pressure kept going up and up. "There's got to be another drug trial. Something really experimental? Seriously, Doc—"

"Seriously, you've got to stop relying on drugs and make

some life changes. You're three breaths away from a stroke, and before you ask…" He started flipping through Roger's chart. "You've tried every medication possible, and some that I think were positively ludicrous. Looks like I'm your third doctor…"

"Fourth if you count the drug-trial people."

His doctor sighed. "Look, I can't even clear you to fly as a passenger in an airplane."

Roger waved that away. "They never check that anyway."

"Not the point."

Roger closed his eyes and tried to remain calm. Sadly, the sight that came to his mind's eye was his father in a treatment facility after his stroke. He hadn't died like Roger's uncle and grandfather, but he had lost the use of a third of his body. Roger tried to force away the panic that skated through his system. "I feel fine," he said firmly.

"Do I need to outline all the reasons high blood pressure is called the *silent* killer?"

No, he didn't need to hear that lecture again. "Okay, so what are my options?"

"Tell me about your exercise and diet."

He knew this drill backward and forward, but he dutifully went through the litany. "I swim a mile and a half most mornings, I don't eat red meat too often, and I know moldy bread does not count as a vegetable. Or olives in martinis."

"Tell me about your job."

Roger barely restrained his groan. "I love my job. I'm the CFO at a robotics firm owned by my best friend. He's the brilliant inventor, I'm the business guy. I make sure his ideas get to market—"

"You do everything, run everything, worry about everything and the stress is killing you."

"I'm not under pressure like those guys," he said firmly.

"They're the geniuses who have to perform miracles every day."

His doctor leaned back in his chair. "So you're surrounded by geniuses under stress. No pressure there. No trying to keep up with their brilliant minds, no struggling against the meltdown of the day, no agony of trying to herd a zillion übersmart cats."

Roger shut his mouth, fighting to keep his expression neutral. Yeah, he often felt like he was the only sane one in a freak show. Other times, he was just the dumb one in charge. His IQ was high, just not stratospheric high. Which at RFE meant he was a moron. "But I love my job," he repeated.

The doctor sighed. "What about meditation? Yoga? There are some interesting guided prayers…"

Roger rolled his eyes. He couldn't help himself. So his doctor switched tracks.

"Look, you've run out of medical options. Do you understand? There's nothing more I can do. You have to make some life changes."

Roger threw up his hands. "Got any suggestions other than quitting my job?"

"Well, when was your last vacation?"

"Just a little bit ago. I went skiing in Colorado. At Christmas."

"Christmas, as in nine months ago?"

"Um, I think so." Or maybe it was two years and nine months ago.

"Take another vacation, Roger. Take it now."

Roger nodded, wondering where in the hell he was going to fit a vacation into his work schedule. "Okay, a vacation. What else?"

"Change your life. Find out what stress is killing you and fix it."

"But—"

"Whatever it takes, Roger. Do it *now*."

THERE WAS SOMETHING really rewarding in being a fill-in office-plant girl, Dr. Amber Smithson thought as she watered a tastefully trimmed fern. Mandolin Hospital hadn't had greenery, or at least none that she remembered. Back then, Amber had thought her work environment was clean and simple. Now she realized it had just been sterile and dead. Which was why she got a special thrill now out of helping corporate America find some green life in a very non-green world.

This wasn't her real job. It was just a way to make ends meet and help out the real plant lady—Mary—who was in bed right now suffering from an extremely painful spell of rheumatoid arthritis. Mary was a good friend who couldn't afford to lose her plant job. So Amber filled in, got to play with plants and, best of all, got to remind herself why she had left the high-pressure life of high-end medicine.

Right now she was in the lobby of RFE, a robotics firm with high-dollar products and mega-dollar research. Pressure was in the very air up here, just like it had been at Mandolin. They might not be working on human bodies, but they were gambling with big money and big ideas. No one could afford to fail and Amber could taste the edge of panic that infected the air. Just like it had at Mandolin.

But she was well free of that, right? she asked herself. For the last two years, she'd been exploring alternative medicine just like she'd always wanted. No one talked to her about liability, no insurance company told her how to treat a patient, and—sadly—no one paid her bills.

Yes, she'd survived all on her own, but her patients were more likely to pay in apple pie than in dollars. Her bank account was getting tight, and her family would only help out if she gave up all her "nonsense" and came back to traditional medicine—preferably at Mandolin. Up until now, she'd refused. But all too soon, an empty bank account was going to force her to make a difficult compromise.

But that wasn't a problem to be faced now. No, right now was for plants, RFE and...yes!...Mr. Roger Martell. The CFO of RFE had just walked into the building, and Amber was perfectly perched behind a planter to spy on the gorgeous man.

He'd caught her eye months ago, when Amber had first subbed as plant girl. Hell, the man caught *every* woman's eye. Tall, dark, stylish and a power executive in every way, Amber'd been secretly spying on him whenever she worked as plant girl. Just being in the same room with him made the air feel electric, as if every second of his day was filled with important decisions. God, he was everything she missed about her old life—the urgency, the power and the feeling that she was doing something vitally important. That was Roger's aura in a nutshell, and naturally, he'd barely stepped into the front lobby when the receptionist started buzzing people.

"Roger's back," the woman said into the phone. "Yes, I'll let him know." She didn't hang up as she handed the man a stack of pink message notes. "Ginny wants to meet with you in a half hour—"

"Hour and a half, at the earliest."

The receptionist didn't miss a beat as she spoke into the phone. "It'll be an hour and a half, Ginny. He knows it's urgent." She hung up the phone and passed him two large manila envelopes.

"Jesus," he moaned. "I was only gone an hour."

"It was a busy hour," the receptionist returned.

Amber had to choke back her laugh as she stretched up to reach a planter hanging from the ceiling. Boy, did she remember those days! There was a time she couldn't take a lunch break without returning to messages, mail and a group of anxious people pacing in the waiting room. She would have guessed that Mr. Martell thrived on the stress until he set down his pile of mail and took a deep calming breath. A big inhale that expanded his chest and filled out his expensive suit, before a slow exhale. And then, damn, a killer smile as he focused on the receptionist.

"So, Claire, how's it going with the new boyfriend? Did he like that wine I recommended?"

The receptionist blinked as if she were stunned by the question, but she recovered fast enough. Then she flashed her own dimples. "Wine, no. Restaurant, yes. He's taking me there tomorrow night."

"Make sure he pays. You're too beautiful to tolerate anything less than royal treatment." Then he paused, abruptly frowning. "Wait a minute. I promised you a dinner there, didn't I? For coming in on Saturday last month to help me with that grant application."

The receptionist bit her lip. "I didn't mind, you know."

"Yeah, but Tommy did, didn't he?"

The girl shrugged. "Tommy has to learn to make sacrifices for my career."

Roger flashed her another quick but devastatingly handsome smile. "That he does. You're an up-and-comer, to be sure. But since I promised you a dinner, I mean to pay up." He pulled out his BlackBerry and hit a quick number. Twenty seconds later, he was speaking to the maitre d'. A minute after that, he snapped the phone shut with a grin. "You're all set. Best table in the house, complimentary champagne and dinner is on me. They already have my credit card, and they'll just add on the tip."

Amber was stunned enough to peer around the fern, her estimation of the man upping by a thousand percent. Corporate promises like "I'll buy you dinner sometime" happened all the time. But no one ever paid up. Except for this guy. Not surprisingly, the receptionist was equally surprised.

"Really, Roger, that's not necessary."

He shrugged, the motion tightening as he caught sight of

an engineer barreling down the hallway at him. "Of course it is, Claire. I promised, and you earned it. Just make sure to toast me at least once."

"You're the best, Roger," the woman breathed. And then they were out of time as the engineer made it to the front desk.

"Roger!" the man barked as he waved a stack of printouts in the air. "Have you seen these specs? Do you know what this is going to cost?"

"Calm down," Roger returned and they began to move together down the hallway. Amber watched him go, appreciating the way his tailored suit accented his lean body.

"God, I love a man in a good suit," she breathed, her voice low enough that only the receptionist could hear.

"Yeah, me, too," responded Claire in an equally quiet tone. "Too bad he's gay."

Amber snapped her head around. "What?" No way was that guy gay. He exuded too much testosterone.

"Yup, queer as folk."

"I don't believe it."

"It's true."

"Why? Just because he dresses nice?"

"It's more than that!" Claire returned. She glanced down the hallway where Roger and the engineer were talking, still in view, but thankfully out of earshot. "Every woman in this company has made a run at him, me included. We've got all types here—brainy, busty, blonde and brunette. We've even got classy and the not-so-classy."

"He never took a bite?"

"Not even a nibble."

Amber shook her head. "That just means he knows better than to play where he works."

"Yeah, but he goes to all these chichi parties, always with gorgeous women."

"So?"

"So one of us always makes a point to find out afterward. You know, are they dating, what's going on, and—"

"And they always say they're friends." Amber released a low laugh. "Honey, that doesn't mean he's gay. Just selective." And probably very discreet.

"Trust me," returned Claire, her voice confident. "No man is that virtuous. Unless he's gay."

Amber shook her head. "Let me give you a hint," she said. "That man right there is a player, high-end executive type. Quiet. Discreet. But hot as they come."

They both turned together to ogle him some more. He was still in deep discussion just down the hallway. The engineer was getting emotional, waving his printouts, gesturing wildly and pointing at a room marked Lab. In contrast, Roger listened seriously, his body taut, but his expression calm. And when the engineer finished speaking, Roger simply shook his head. Not surprisingly, the engineer got more frantic while Roger became more still. In the end, the engineer stormed off in a huff which left Roger time to look up and flash both Amber and Claire a rueful smile before moving down the hall.

Claire huffed. "Definitely gay."

"Discreet, type A and hetero through and through." Amber leaned back against the counter and sighed as a wave of memories hit. "Trust me on this. I know his type."

Claire gave her an arch look, making sure to scan her shapeless sundress and cheap sandals. "I'm sure you think—"

"You think I grew up wearing flip-flops and a tank? I spent my youth dating guys like that. My father was an executive just like him. And my mother runs the cardiology ward at a top hospital. I was surrounded by the type."

"And then?" Claire asked, obviously wondering how she'd gone from the silver spoon life to filling in as the plant girl.

Amber shrugged. "I burned out on the politics. I couldn't

get anything done except for what *they* wanted, so I went rogue. Doesn't mean I don't remember though. And let me tell you—sex with the alpha dog?" She sighed. "That's one hot ride."

Claire frowned, but then her eyes abruptly widened. "Wait a moment. I know you! Mary told me all about you."

Amber winced. "Don't believe everything Mary says."

"No! She told me you'd be filling in. You're that doctor! You run a free clinic out in that artsy area of Chicago. What's it called?"

"Cherry Hills, not that there are any cherries or hills anywhere near. And it's really not that artsy." More like converted warehouses. The neighborhood artistes gloried in their studio lofts, but the population included more reformed drug addicts and single mothers than wannabe Picassos. Like her, everyone in Cherry Hills was just at the edge of poverty, struggling to keep it together.

"And you're Doc Crystal!"

"My name's Amber. They just thought it was a crystal and the name stuck..." she began, trying divert the discussion. But it was too late. Claire was off and running.

"Yeah! Doc Crystal. You're like this doctor Robin Hood and Mother Teresa all rolled into one. Mary says you're amazing!"

"Mary's on massive painkillers. And I, um, gotta get back to these plants." Amber turned away. She hated the hero worship that appeared in people's eyes the minute they heard "free clinic" and "doctor" in the same sentence. That's why she let people think she had a corporate background rather than high-end medicine. In her mind, they were one and the same, but for other people? There was a world of difference.

As for running a free clinic, her neighbor couldn't afford a doctor, so he had come visiting one night. And then another neighbor and another. Before she knew it, she had regular patients. They didn't care that she wasn't affiliated with any hospital or clinic. They needed help she could give, and her services were free.

Meanwhile, Claire was following her around, her lips pursed in thought and a mercenary look in her eye. "How sure are you that Roger's straight?"

Amber blinked. That wasn't what she'd expected the woman to ask. But she answered anyway. "One hundred percent straight."

"Prove it."

"What? How?"

"Think you could get him to kiss you?"

Amber frowned. Well, she'd been fantasizing about just that possibility for weeks now. She'd even figured out a way to approach him, but she'd never thought she'd actually implement the plan. But Claire wasn't to be deterred.

"I'll bet you a double mochaccino that you can't."

Amber laughed. "I don't drink coffee."

Claire rolled her eyes. "Of course you don't. Okay, how about this? I'll get you a half-dozen of those big vegan muffins that Mary loves."

Ooh, now there was a temptation. Amber had heard about those muffins. And truthfully, she had been thinking about arranging a meeting with Roger Martell for a while now. She thought RFE's product line was very interesting and knew Jack might be intrigued as well. Yes, Jack, her once best friend and—a very, very long time ago—her lover. They'd kept in touch over the last two years. He'd call and try and tempt her back to Mandolin. She'd never been interested before, but now, thanks to near poverty, she was beginning to consider it.

She could meet with Roger, arrange for the introduction with Jack, and use the conversation to discreetly find out how things stood at Mandolin. She didn't really want to admit it, but two years as a rogue researcher was wearing on her.

Maybe if things had changed at the hospital, she'd consider going back.

And if she managed to wrangle a kiss from Roger at the same time, well, a girl could dream. She'd been two years out in the cold in her sex life, too. She knew just how to attract his attention, although she'd have to dig to the very back of her closet to find the clothes. And God only knew what had happened to her makeup. But still, it would be fun to play. Just a little kiss. What would be the harm?

"Well?" pressed Claire.

"Deal."

3

ROGER WAS CURSING at his watch when Claire buzzed him. Then he cursed again at the buzz because it was after seven on a Friday and he had to leave.

"Hey, Roger, you have a moment? I've got someone who needs five minutes of your time."

"This is a really bad time, Claire," he said. "Sam's bachelor party's starting in less than an hour. I've got to—"

"Five minutes," interrupted a woman's voice that he'd never heard before. It was low and precise, like from a sexy accountant. A sexy accountant? What the hell was he thinking?

"I really haven't—"

"I'll make it worth your while," the unknown woman said, and this time there was no accountant in the tone, just pure sex. "I've got some ideas about your newest product that I think could make both of us very happy."

That caught his attention. RFE was desperate for new markets. Robotics companies couldn't survive on building a walking, talking robot like most people imagined. No one could really afford something like that. But attach a robotic arm to a wheelchair, and suddenly things got more interesting. Connect high-tech robotics to a prosthetic, and amputees started expressing interest. And given the state of the economy, he couldn't afford to turn away any possibilities.

"Five minutes," he grumbled as he powered down his laptop. He'd talk to the woman as he prepared to leave for Sam's party. The wedding wasn't for a month yet, but packed schedules had pushed up the date to tonight. And as best man, Roger wanted to get there early to make sure everything was the way it ought to be. He'd ordered booze, strippers and the best nachos money could buy. Sam wouldn't notice any of it—he was head over heels in love with Julie—but it was the principle of the thing. As best man, it was incumbent upon Roger to see that things were done right.

Then his thoughts stuttered to a halt as Claire showed a woman into his office. Not just a woman, but class in a pencil skirt and stiletto ankle boots. He straightened up from his desk to look closer. She was average height with light brown hair done up in a polished lift, but everything else about her throbbed with power. Not he-woman power, but corporate slick—the tasteful, expensive kind. Her suit and shoes were understated but of the finest quality. But what really got his attention was that she moved with a swaying precision that told him she could be completely business...or not.

And, wow, one part of him was very interested in the "not" side. Geez, even her scent—a simple lemon smell, he thought—had his dick lifting with desire. When was the last time that happened? No one had piqued his interest this fast since he'd first hit puberty. Thankfully, he was older now and could tell his libido to back down. At least he tried. Until she did the absolutely perfect move to pique his lust. She turned to Claire and smiled, instantly transforming her face from cool corporate to warm girl next door.

"Thanks, Claire. And thank you for the muffins," she said as she lifted a box.

"They're for Mary. You have to earn yours," Claire returned with a grin.

"I know," the woman answered.

Roger struggled to keep his libido from completely taking over his brain. "Um, sorry, but I really don't have a lot of time," he said as he snapped his briefcase shut. Then he cursed. He'd left his calendar out on his desk. He'd been searching through it, looking for a way to fit in a vacation. A couple days or a long weekend. Something. But he'd already looked three months out and he had nothing. Maybe the doctor was right. Maybe he needed to quit his job. But the idea of doing that just killed him inside.

The woman handed over her business card. "I won't take up much of your time, I swear," she said.

Before he could answer, Claire spoke up. "I've got to get home, Roger. I'm going to lock up the front, so you'll have to leave through the lab. You're the last ones here, so kill the lights, too, okay?"

"No problem. Have a nice weekend," Roger replied as he inspected his visitor's business card. "Dr. Amber Smithson," he read out loud. "From Mandolin Hospital and Clinic." He looked up, intrigued. She sure as hell didn't look like any doctor he knew, but then he'd never been to the prestigious Mandolin either. "What brings you to Chicago?"

The woman sat down in a chair and treated him to the delicious view of her skirt creeping up as she crossed her legs. The sight was so mesmerizing, he almost missed what she said.

"Oh, this and that," she answered vaguely.

"Publicity, donations, benefit gala?" he asked. That was the usual reason someone like her came to Chicago. Just as he spent much of his time hitting those events, trying to connect up with the movers and shakers in medicine, looking for ways to get robotic equipment to the people who could benefit from it the most.

"Not this trip," she said with a smile. "But you've managed to catch my eye nonetheless."

He put his calendar inside his briefcase, then leaned a hip against his desk. "Okay, Dr. Smithson—"

"Amber, please."

"All right, Amber. You've got my attention. What is it that you're looking for?"

She arched a brow. "I have a friend who might be interested in a face-to-face with the power behind RFE. Your company has an interesting if rather scattered product line. But there are possibilities…"

He raised his hands in an apologetic gesture. "Sam's not here right now, but I'm sure we could make an appointment…" His words trailed off as she arched a sculpted eyebrow.

"Please. I've heard about Mr. Finn. He might be the genius engineer, but you're the corporate backbone. Trust me when I say I'd much rather be talking to you. He'll have to come to the meeting, of course, but you're the business guy. And as we both know, medicine is big business."

He nodded slowly. It was true—all of it. Sam and he had been best friends since grade school, and together they had built RFE. But Sam was the visionary. Roger was the business guy who made it all come true. "You seem to know a lot about my company."

Her smile was slow, but no less seductive. "I did my research. You've got quite the interesting place here."

Wow, she was beautiful when she smiled. He wasn't even sure exactly what had him so hot. Piece by piece, she was not drop-dead gorgeous. She wasn't even wearing any makeup to speak of. But she had a glow about her, a warmth and a vitality that really grabbed hold of him.

Beep-beep! Beep-beep!

His watch alarm interrupted an extremely inappropriate train of thought. Thank God. He tapped the button, then smiled his apology to Dr. Amber Smithson. She nodded, pushed to her feet in a single lithe motion and extended her hand. "You have to go. It was good to meet you, Mr. Martell."

"How long are you in town?" he suddenly asked. He didn't have time for an elaborate dance of maybe this, maybe that. But he could invest an evening or two.

"I'm not entirely sure," she answered. "This is kind of a spur-of-the-moment diversion for me." She glanced at him, her look significant, though damned if he understood why. "My interest in your company is real, Mr. Martell, but I do have an ulterior motive. I hope you're okay with that."

He laughed. He already knew she had an ulterior motive. No woman who looked like her landed in his lap for no reason. There was always a price tag attached. "We're in the preliminary dance. I got that." He looked at his watch again. "And I also have to go."

"Of course," she said. "Okay if I walk out with you?"

He smiled. "Fine with me. I'll show you the executive elevator."

She preceded him out of his office door. "I'm all aquiver."

Maybe, he thought with a grin, and maybe not. The "executive elevator" was really a lab elevator, extra large with no frills attached. It was used for moving heavy equipment, but it was also fast, private and emptied out near his car.

He watched her closely for her reaction to the stripped-down conveyance. Would she turn up her lip at the lack of polished brass and glass?

Nope. When the elevator doors opened and revealed its undignified glory, she merely raised her eyebrows in surprise then flashed him her warm smile. Like the one she'd given Claire earlier, it was filled with humanity and amusement. As if he were getting a glimpse of the woman beneath the suit. And it was a glimpse that he liked.

They entered the elevator and while he hit the button for the garage, she tapped her toe on the rubber flooring. "Frills on the outside, no nonsense on the inside. I'm liking your company more and more, Mr. Martell."

"Glad to hear—"

Grind.

That was the elevator gears, making a horrible sound. It was loud and grating, and they both looked up in anxious surprise.

Thunk!

The elevator dropped a half inch and stopped with a jerk.

He stumbled slightly, but kept his footing. Dr. Smithson, on the other hand, had on stiletto heels. She practically fell over. He caught her, of course. What else would any red-blooded man do? She grabbed his arms, he tightened his grip and a split second later they were full-body pressed together. He had the predictable reaction, especially when she looked up at him with wide, startled eyes.

"What just happened?" she gasped.

It took an effort to separate his mind and his libido, but eventually he managed it. She'd recovered her footing, so there was no need for him to be pressed up against her. But, damn, she felt so soft and womanly. He had to force himself to straighten his arms and step away.

He already knew by feel that the elevator was dead, but he crossed to the panel and pushed the button anyway. Then he switched to pressing the call button for building maintenance. Except it was after seven on a Friday night. No one was around to answer.

With a soft curse, he whipped open his BlackBerry and hit the first number in his speed dial. Sadly, his best friend was no more responsive than building maintenance. Hell. When the call went to voice mail, he grumbled a quick, "Sam! We're stuck in your damned elevator. Call me and tell me how to fix this *now!*" Then he shut the phone with an angry clench of his fist, his mind already scrambling to worst-case scenarios. He was going to miss the bachelor party. He might very well be stuck in this elevator all night. One look at his companion, and he found that he couldn't quite call that a loss. But he had yet to see how she reacted under stress. A woman like her had to have evening plans.

She stared back at him, her lips already curving into a rueful grimace. "You're joking, right? We're stuck here? Seriously?"

"Sam's been tinkering with this thing. Wanted to make some special modifications before the wedding next month." He held up his hand. "Don't ask because I don't know. I'm the stupid one here, engineering-wise. The point is that no one is available to rescue us, most especially not my best friend who is headed to his bachelor party across town. A party, I might add, that I'm hosting but am now going to miss unless I can get said best friend to answer his phone."

"Wow," she said as her eyebrows rose and her eyes lit with humor. "Wow, that really sucks." Except it didn't sound like she was upset. In fact, if anything, it looked like she was on the verge of laughter.

He arched a brow. "Is there something I'm missing here?"

"No, no," she said. "The universe does work in interesting ways, doesn't it?"

"Um, what?"

She lifted her face toward him, and it was definitely true. She was holding back great big belly laughs. "You're telling me that we're trapped here, alone in this elevator, with no one in the building. In fact, we're probably stuck here for like an hour or more."

He frowned at her, wondering if this was a weird stress reaction. It didn't seem like that, but he'd never met a business woman who *laughed* at a schedule change. Their life—his life—was built too tight for that.

"Well," he said, "I know I could call 911 or something, but as this is Sam's private elevator, I'd hate to have them bust through a panel when Sam probably can just phone me a fix."

"No, no," she said, waving a hand in the air. "Don't bother." Her voice was still trembling with laughter.

"I don't understand—"

She abruptly stepped closer and pressed her fingers to his lips, cutting off his next words. "You don't have to understand, Mr. Martell. I think the universe is just arranging things for me. Which makes me feel incredibly guilty because I haven't exactly been honest with you."

He did not like the sound of that. Straightening, he gently but firmly removed her hand from his face. His libido objected strongly, but at this particular moment, his brain was in charge. "I don't like lies, Dr. Smithson."

"I don't blame you." She flashed a rueful smile. "And I haven't lied so much as not confessed my ulterior motive."

He folded his arms across his chest and arched a brow. "Yes?"

"It has to do with a bet."

4

"DID YOU KNOW THAT Claire thinks you're gay?" Amber pushed the words out in a rush, and she wasn't surprised when it took a moment for Roger to process the information. But when he did, his body jerked in shock.

"What?"

She could see his mind spinning a mile a minute, so she rushed out her side of the story before he could imagine something worse. "She said you were gay, I said no way and so we have a bet going."

He gaped at her, but as she expected, he caught up quickly. "This is a seduction? Did you tamper with the elevator?"

His tone was less than flattering, and she reacted purely on instinct. "Of course not!"

His eyes narrowed. "To which? The seduction or the tampering?"

She grimaced, but he had her there. She hadn't meant this to be a seduction—well, not in an elevator at this particular moment—but this had been an elaborate game of foreplay. "I'm a doctor, not an engineer. I wouldn't know how to stop an elevator if my life depended on it."

He wasn't fooled. "And the seduction?"

"It was just for a kiss," she confessed. "And now I've told

you without making any moves. I just…I just thought it was funny that the universe somehow maneuvered us into a stalled elevator at just the right time." Her words trailed away on a lame note. Great. Some seductress she'd turned out to be. Meanwhile, his eyes weren't narrowed anymore. His expression was more one of deep thought.

"What was the prize?"

She blinked. Beyond getting to kiss the alpha executive? "Um…" She pointed to the box of baked goods. "More of those."

He snorted. "I don't know whether to be flattered or insulted. Seriously, my kisses are worth a box of muffins?"

"Well, they are *vegan* muffins," she clarified.

"Does that make it better or worse?"

She smiled. Okay, so he wasn't furious. Which left them exactly where? She might have called everything off when she was in her shapeless sundress and hemp sandals. But she was dressed for success right now, in her last surviving power suit. Clothes did make a difference and part of her really missed the woman who was climbing the Mandolin corporate ladder, seeing a zillion patients and trying to change the course of medicine one closed mind at a time. She'd had purpose then, and she'd been helping people. What had she done lately but feed her own intellect?

"Are you even a doctor?" he asked.

She nodded. "And I really did work at Mandolin."

At his skeptical look, she reached into her purse. She didn't have a fancy BlackBerry like she'd once had permanently attached to her body, but she did have a massively cheap prepaid. She dialed the number from memory, then put it on speaker so that Mr. Martell could hear the conversation. The switchboard answered on the second ring.

"Mandolin Hospital, how may I be of service?"

"Please connect me to Dr. Jack Ross. It's Dr. Amber Smithson about a consult." Then she rattled off his extension.

Across from her, Roger frowned and looked at his watch. Amber just laughed.

"We always stayed late on Friday nights. We shut our doors, pretended we'd gone home, then got a ton of work done. Plus, it covered for the fact that we had no social life except for our jobs."

As expected, Jack answered on the second ring.

"Amber?" A low voice rumbled through the line. "Has a miracle happened? Have you finally decided to give up all your pie-eyed idealism? I've been working on the director since you left. He might be open to you coming back, but only if you schmooze him right."

Amber barely held back her smile. This was exactly what she wanted to hear. But she couldn't seem too eager, so she glanced at her elevator companion. "Hello, Jack. Look, I've got you on speaker with a Roger Martell of RFE. That stands for Robotics For Everyone."

As she spoke, Roger pulled out his BlackBerry. A glance at his screen showed that he was looking up Jack's pedigree. A second later his eyebrows rose. Yup, Jack was one impressive neurologist. But more important, his work with amputees made him an ideal consultant to a robotics company.

Jack was groaning into the phone. "Jeez, Amber, not another robotics firm. I've got them coming out of my ears."

"Would I steer you wrong? Just give them an hour. Let them prove their worth."

Jack took a long time to answer, but in the end, he groaned his agreement. "Fine. I have an hour first Tuesday next month. Bring him then."

She grinned at Roger. "It'll be two of them. Roger Martell and Sam Finn—"

"And you, Amber. You bring them in person or not at all."

Perfect. Exactly what she'd wanted in the first place. "Fine," she said with a pretend show of reluctance. "If that's the only way."

"Tuesday at three. With you or not at all." With that, Jack cut the connection.

Amber exhaled and slowly clicked her phone shut. She didn't know what to think about what she'd just done. It felt like the outfit, plus having her hair piled on top of her head again, had somehow put her back in time. She was Dr. Smithson again, thinking nothing of scheduling a meeting halfway across the country. It felt strange, but also good. She'd never felt more powerful than when she was in this mode. It was seductive, this feeling, and she worried that she was compromising too much. Then she remembered her bank account and knew that some compromises were necessary.

Meanwhile, Roger was looking at her as a man might take the measure of a cobra. "So you're on the level," he said, though it came out part question.

"That part was real, yes."

"And the seduction part?" he prompted, his tone annoyingly neutral.

She shrugged, but she couldn't resist putting a little attitude into the movement. She'd never had to beg for sex before, she sure as hell wasn't going to start now. "As I said, the universe works in mysterious ways."

"That's not an answer," he said.

"It wasn't meant to be."

He paused, his eyes too dark, his expression very intense and completely unreadable. And then he took a slow step forward. "And you think I'm gay."

"That was Claire. I'm betting a half-dozen vegan muffins on straight." She arched a brow. Any man with his looks would have an ego to go with it. And, my, she loved teasing a man with an ego. "Straight, hard and so hot sometimes even you can't stand it."

His lips curved in a predatory smile. "Takes one to know one."

She laughed, the sound coming out low and throaty without her consciously willing it. "Just because I recognize a fellow playmate doesn't mean I'm going to dance in your sandbox."

"And yet you made a bet with Claire, dressed up all pretty for me and strutted your way into my office."

"I didn't stop the elevator. Maybe you did."

He shook his head, and she would swear his eyes glittered with sexual intent. "How does a single kiss prove that I'm straight?" He moved closer, his attitude part anger, part dominance and all male. It was only years of training that kept her standing still. Most women would be backing up as he tightened the distance between them. Within a moment she could feel the heat of his breath across her skin.

"That was the bet," she said. "One kiss. If you want to fake it, that's up to you."

"I'm not going to fake anything," he growled.

The air seemed to tingle as it entered her lungs, and her skin flushed with heat. Without even planning it, her chin shot up and she met him stare for stare. But she couldn't speak as he came so close to her lips.

"One kiss?" he whispered. He brushed his mouth against her cheek in what was definitely a kiss. It made her whole body shiver. "Was that a kiss?" he asked. He shifted to nip the tip of her nose. "Or how about this?"

Finally, he made it to her mouth. While she held her breath in anticipation, he brushed a single, long, thorough kiss across her lips. No tongue, just his lips. And it was the hottest thing she'd experienced in nearly two years.

He was toying with her, getting her hot without fulfilling her bet or her personal hunger. This was what came of playing with an alpha dog. But she wasn't without skills of her own.

"Yes," she whispered, as she stretched up on her toes to let her breath warm his mouth. "That'll count." Then she forced herself to drop back on her heels and step away.

He arched his brow at her, a challenge in his eye. "Glad I could be of service. You let me know if you need some more proof."

She grinned. "Is that an invitation to play?"

She watched him pause a moment, and then his expression slid to pure male. "Yeah, it is. Did you have something else in mind?"

And there was the gauntlet thrown down in challenge. Did she have the nerve to pick it up? It had been two years since she'd played any type of sex game with anyone. Two years since she'd put on stilettos and done up her hair. Two years of burying her nose in every type of bizarre holistic treatment she could find. And none of it had been as fun as this moment right now. So did she go for it? All the way?

How could she not? After two years, she was beyond ready.

She stretched her hands up in the air and slowly pulled out the pins holding her hair in place. She knew he was watching her, so she worked as slowly and as seductively as possible. And then, when she was sure he was good and caught, she flashed him a wink. "There's a Tantric game I've always wanted to play," she said.

He swallowed, but that was the only indication she'd affected him. Well, that and the bulge down below. "A game?" he rasped.

She stepped right up to him, leaned in close and moved

her lips to his left ear. She even pressed a hand to his chest so she could feel his heart beat under her palm.

"He who comes first, loses."

He released a growl, low in his belly. Like a great beast coming awake after a long sleep, and at the sound, she knew she had him.

"Sounds like a good game," he said as his hands slid around her waist. "You think I'm going to play with you? You think I'm going to risk a potential deal with Mandolin just to get you in bed?"

"I do." She nipped at his earlobe with her teeth.

"And why would I do that?"

"Because I got your attention," she said as she thumbed open two buttons on his dress shirt and slipped a finger inside. There was a light dusting of hair there, just enough to be manly without detracting from the muscle she felt beneath his skin.

"Lots of women get my attention."

His hands began creeping upward toward her breasts. Her nipples tightened and her breath caught and held. She'd forgotten how hot this was. How absolutely incredible it was to just let go.

"Yeah, but I'm the only one stuck in an elevator with you."

He chuckled and the rumble of his body was like a low throb in her own. "True."

And then there was a moment's pause. His hands stilled, and so did her own. They both stopped teasing, stopped tempting, stopped everything as a single question filtered through the air: Were they really going to do this? His gaze caught hers and they communicated silently. Was this worth the risk?

"Do you have a condom?" he asked.

"In my purse." Then she glanced around the freight elevator. "Any cameras?"

"Nope. And I've got a clean bill of health."

"Me, too."

His smile was slow in coming, but it was all the more devastating because of it. The man was *potent*. His nostrils had flared, his hands were strong and he was physically backing her up against the wall. And just when she thought he'd pounce, he held himself back and waited while her breath stuttered in and out of her chest.

"He who comes first loses?" he asked.

"That's the game."

"And what do I get if I win?"

She let her hands slide down until she was stroking the very long, large length of him. "You get invited to round two."

"I like the sound of that." He paused for effect, then moved an inch closer. "Game on."

He wasn't subtle in going for it, not that she expected him to be. His hands slid to the back of her skirt and, within a second, she felt the zipper slide down, then her skirt dropped to the floor. She was standing in her thong and thigh-highs. If she were going to back out, this was the one move guaranteed to make her run for the hills.

She didn't. In fact, she kicked the fabric away while she undid the buttons on his shirt. She meant to act strong but her fingers were trembling and she fumbled with the last buttons. Or perhaps it had more to do with the way he was stroking her thighs, running his fingertips along the edge of her hose before cupping her backside.

God, he had good hands, firm and large enough to support her as she wrapped one leg around him to pull him tight. So they could press heat to heat despite the fabric between them. Lord, he felt so good that she thought about impaling herself right then and there. She wanted him deep inside her; she wanted to be stretched to the very limit.

With that thought in mind, she went to the button of his

trousers, but her fingers were too clumsy and there wasn't enough space as he pushed her firmly against the padded wall. A second later, he was pressing his full body against hers, trapping her fingers. Her hands were useless as he began to thrust, groin to groin, over and over in a steadily building rhythm.

Oh, unfair! she thought. Her hands were pinned but his were free to pop open the buttons of her blouse. The black lace bra beneath had a front clasp, and so it took no time at all for him to free her breasts. He filled his hands with her and began to squeeze in just the right ways. She let her head drop back as hunger shuddered through her body.

Her heart thrummed, her skin flushed hot and her breath came in tight gasps as he manipulated her nipples. She didn't remember ever having the desire build so fast before. He couldn't be able to make her come without even pulling down his pants!

He bent down to put his mouth on her breasts. She knew without a doubt that if he was as skilled there as he seemed to be everywhere else, then she'd lose their little game within seconds. He was that good—or it had been that long for her. Either way, she wasn't going to give up that easily. With a sudden surge of strength, she freed her hands and shoved him away.

He stumbled backward. Not far, but enough that she could take some measure of control back. Dispensing with the niceties, she grabbed either side of his shirt and yanked. Buttons popped off and his shirt was halfway down his arms in a single motion.

His eyes widened as he looked down at first himself, then at her. "That is the hottest thing I've ever seen," he said.

She grinned. She'd guessed he liked women who could match him power for power. Clearly she was right. With another yank, she had the shirt all the way down to his wrists, but the cuffs caught and held.

"Take it off the rest of the way," she ordered, "or I'll just rip it."

He shook his head, his white teeth flashing again. "You're not that strong."

She arched her brow. "It'll hurt."

His grin widened, so she took the challenge. She jerked as hard as she could, but the fabric was stronger than she expected. As she was busy hauling on his shirt, he used her movement to spin her around and trap her backward against his chest. And worse, his shirt now held her captive whereas he had an arm free to stroke her.

If it were only his free hand caressing her shoulder, her breasts, her belly, she would have had less trouble resisting him. But then he did something no man had ever done to her before. His lips found the back of her neck. Not just the base of her skull but lower along her spine, as his chin pushed her blouse aside.

She felt his breath across her skin, the stroke of his lips as he teased her flesh, and then the slight scrape of teeth before the soothing circle of his tongue. On her neck and all the way down to between her shoulder blades. Her entire nervous system went limp with delight. God, never before had a man found that zone and used it to his advantage like that.

The wave was upon her before she even knew it was coming. She cried out in shock as she lost control of her body. Waves of pleasure rolled through her. They were sudden and wild and the best orgasm she'd had in years.

Thank God, he held her through it all, his arms firm, his stance solid. She might have collapsed onto the floor in an undignified, boneless heap otherwise. But he was a gentleman, supporting her as she writhed in his arms. And when she finally recovered, when she at last found enough strength to settle her feet beneath her, only then did she look up to his face. He'd won their bet, and so she expected to see a very male smirk. She didn't. His expression was open in surprise. She might even have said he looked dazed.

She twisted, her legs still wobbly. But before she could ask her question, he swooped down to kiss her. It was a deep kiss, but it was also gentle, almost reverent.

"You're amazing," he said. "That was…amazing. I've never seen a woman look so hot when she comes."

She didn't know how to answer. After all, she was the one who'd just come without even stepping out of her thong. He was the one with the incredible mouth. And now, when she was obviously speechless with shock, his smile did shift to a cat-ate-the-canary grin. And then he slowly unwound her from his shirt.

"Name it," he said when she was standing directly before him.

She blinked. "Name what?"

"The time and place for round two."

5

ROGER DIDN'T TRY to hide his grin as Amber struggled to find her dignity. She needn't bother. He thought her the sexiest thing alive just as she was. She had that cool exterior, but she'd come apart in his arms. Just from what he'd done to her neck. And didn't that just make him feel like a major stud?

It didn't even bother him that he had a boner the size of the Sears Tower. He was beyond happy—and that was the most bizarre thing given that they were still trapped in this damn elevator.

Meanwhile, Amber blinked at him, her eyes wide with shock. "I never..." she began. "I mean, it's been a while, but never before..." She shook her head, put her hands to her red cheeks and groaned. "I don't know what to say."

She looked so vulnerable that he reached out a finger and stroked just below her left ear. It was all he could touch behind her hands. "You don't have to say anything. It was great. Seriously."

Her hands fell away, and she frowned at him. "Okay, so you *are* gay."

He blinked, his vision of himself as a male stud disappearing by the second. "What?"

"To put it in Claire's words, no man is that virtuous unless he's gay."

He laughed. He hadn't meant to, but just the idea that they had been taking bets on his sexuality seemed funny to him. He was so *not* gay. And to prove it, he grabbed hold of her hand and pressed it hard against his length.

God, that felt good. She knew how to hold a man, even through his trousers. Right pressure, right stroke. His breath shuddered through him and his eyes practically rolled back in his head.

"Not gay," he said. "Want me to prove it?"

"Yes," she breathed, and his eyes snapped open. Her skin was still flushed, but there was definite hunger in her eyes. "God, yes," she repeated when he just stared at her.

He didn't stop this time. He didn't hold himself back, and he sure as hell didn't go easy on her. He had her pressed up against the wall in a second. Her blouse was still open, her bra swinging free, so he could have filled his hands with her breasts. He *wanted* to fill his hands with her breasts because she had great ones. But his hands were too busy dropping his trousers.

Thankfully, she was helping him, her hands shaking as much as his. And when his pants and boxers finally dropped to his ankles, they both released a moan of pleasure.

Her thong was in the way, and he started to peel it down. But she grabbed him by the ears—ouch!—and pulled him eye to eye.

"I ripped yours," she said.

He grinned. "As you wish." Then he grabbed both edges of the lacy elastic and pulled. She watched him do it, her eyes lit with joy.

"That is so hot!" she breathed. Then when he was going to go right back to her, she pressed a hand to his chest. "Condom."

He bent down to his pants and pulled his wallet out, flipping it open to the appropriate pouch. But again she stopped him with a touch, this time on his wrist.

"How long has that been in there?"

He frowned a moment, thinking back. Erg. Much too long. Sure, he had dates with hot women, but it'd been over a year since he'd brought one home with him. "Better go with yours."

She leaned down to get her purse, and he almost came right there. Even though she'd bent her knees in a rather demure pose considering she was naked in all the important parts, he could see the pink rounded curves of her bottom, and knew just how fabulous it would feel to flip her around and drill her from behind.

He didn't. That would be crass. And besides, he didn't have the condom on yet. But he could imagine and stroke those luscious curves as she moved.

She was still bent down when she turned to pass him the foil packet, giving him a mischievous wink. "Like what you see?" she asked. And then, damn if she didn't extend her legs slowly while keeping her head down. Good God, she was flexible!

His hands were shaking as he suited up in record time. To hell with crass. She was giving him the choice, and he took it. It was only a half step to position himself, and then—yes!—a single, deep thrust and he was embedded inside her.

She gasped, her back arching beautifully. But then she gripped him. A long, low squeeze that started at his base and rolled up to the tip. Tight and hard and where had she learned to do that? He made a sound that might have been a growl, and she chuckled right before she did it again.

That was it. His brain fuzzed completely out and there was no stopping him. He grabbed hold of her hips and began to pump. He meant to pay more attention to her pleasure—God knows, he meant a lot of things—but he had no control. Not when she kept squeezing him like that.

And then, sweet heaven, she tumbled over the edge. She arched and cried out. Her grip became impossibly tight before she began to milk him in a strong pull. He slammed into her one last time, then erupted like never before. Holy cow, he even blacked out for a moment. And the pleasure of that release was like nothing he'd ever experienced before. Heaven. Pure heaven!

But it didn't last. It never did. Joy, ecstasy, even that sweet moment of unconsciousness faded away almost instantly. His mind kicked in, his thought resurfaced, and suddenly he realized he was leaning against the wall of a freight elevator still embedded in a woman he'd just met a half hour ago.

God, what was he thinking?

He took a deep breath, trying to gain some control. But even though his brain had kicked back in, his body still needed time to recover. It took a few more breaths before he could lean forward and help Amber stand. She was rather boneless, even in this position, but she moved easily enough. And he, sadly, slipped out of her as they adjusted.

"Mmm," she murmured as she pushed her hair out of her eyes. "I take it back. You're not gay. And if you are, I don't want to know about it."

"I'm not gay," he said with a chuckle. "And I gotta know—does that count as round two or do I get to see you again?" The words were out before his brain could stop him. Did he even want to see her again? Sure, the sex was great, explosive even. But no guy was this lucky. Fabulous, no-strings-attached sex with a woman who looked like her? A woman who could bend over and kiss her own ankles? This was a setup for sure. He just didn't know for what.

She started chewing on her bottom lip. She was uncertain

and feeling awkward. Somehow that reassured him. A setup wouldn't look as sweetly embarrassed as she did.

"I—I, um," she stammered. "I think that was round two. This, uh, this isn't really who I am anymore," she said, gesturing to her thigh-highs and stiletto heels.

He shrugged, his suspicions starting to ease. "It's not who I am either, but damn…"

"It was good, wasn't it?"

He nodded. "Yeah." With repartee like that, he was losing his Mr. Stud status fast. He scrambled to think of something to say that wasn't lame. "Look, we don't have to make it into something big. Just dinner. Very safe. Very casual."

She didn't answer. She began pulling on her skirt and he abruptly felt stupid standing there with his boxers at his ankles. So they both got busy readjusting themselves until they were facing each other fully dressed, and another awkward silence descended.

"So you're a doctor, huh?" And again, he failed to find anything clever to say.

"Um, yeah. Well, no, not really. I mean, there's an MD behind my name but…" She sighed and shrugged. "It's kinda complicated."

He gestured to where they were, stranded in a freight elevator. "I've got some time. How about you?"

"Uh, yeah." She released a laugh. "Okay, personal history—the short version. I used to be this person. I used to be Mandolin Hospital, working toward management, fancy doctor with all the trimmings. Except I never made it. I had this desire to learn about stuff Western medicine didn't encompass. In the end…" She shrugged. "I had to choose."

"And you chose what exactly?"

"Research. The truth is that I have a fundamental need to explore, and the administration had a fundamental need to make me toe the line. I hit a moment when I just couldn't do it anymore."

He folded his arms across his chest and studied her face. He didn't see any signs of outright deception, but she damn well wasn't telling the whole story. No one upended their lives like that without something major happening.

"So you came to Chicago to do what? Let me guess, was there a guy involved?"

"Definitely no guy—I'd broken up with my last boyfriend at least a year earlier. And frankly, I've always been too focused on medicine for relationships. No, I came out here to visit Mary."

When he frowned, not placing the name, she filled in the clues for him.

"She's your plant lady. The one with rheumatoid arthritis. Those muffins are for her," she said, pointing to the box on the floor.

"Ah. Right. Sorry." He remembered, he just couldn't put a face to the name.

"Anyway, she was one of my first patients a long time ago. So when I hopped into my car and started driving, I ended up on her doorstep. And then I stayed."

"Doing what?"

"Besides filling in for her?"

She waited a moment, studying his face for something. In the end, he just raised his hands in surrender. "What am I missing?"

"I'm the fill-in plant lady. You saw me this afternoon after your lunch appointment." As he continued to stare, her lips curled up in a smile. "I knew you didn't recognize me. Picture me like this…" She lifted her hair into a ponytail. "Now add a shapeless sundress and hemp sandals."

It took him a moment, but he got there. And he felt his eyes widen in shock. "Oh, my God! That's you? The baggy plant lady I see sometimes? The one who could be pretty if she just made an effort?" He bit his tongue, then gestured to her clothing. "But then I guess you already know that you're gorgeous when you make the effort."

She waved off the compliment with a too-casual gesture. "I happen to think I'm beautiful even when I don't make the effort. Beauty comes from within."

Roger shook his head. "In your case, beauty comes from inside and outside."

She took the compliment gracefully with a regal nod of her head, but something still didn't sit right. He leaned forward.

"So you've given up medicine all together? Just to water plants?"

She shook her head. "No, no. Like I said, I do research. And before you ask, it's not the kind of research you're thinking of. No laboratory funded by a pharmaceutical grant. No Ph.Ds and definitely no Bunsen burner in sight."

He nodded like he understood her. Which he didn't. "So what kind of research?"

"New age."

It took him a moment to process her words. And even then it was another moment beyond that. Meanwhile, she was cringing. Not obviously. Just a little, as if she expected him to start mocking her. He didn't. During his mother's last year, she'd explored crystals and aromatherapy and more. He never saw that it made any difference except to her. It gave her something to focus on before her death, something to explore. In many ways, he believed it gave his mother some peace before the end. In fact, when she'd finally died, he'd thought she was just meditating there for a moment.

"So you're researching the effects of what? Crystals? Acupressure? Qigong?"

She straightened, obviously surprised that he hadn't started laughing. "I tried those. They haven't produced the results I'm looking for. So I'm looking at other modalities now."

"Such as?"

"Energy healing. No needles. No herbs or crystals. Just—"

"Prayer."

She shrugged. "Some people call it that." She tilted her head. "You sound like you know something about it."

"My mother spent the last year of her life on alternative healing. I got the tour along with her."

"And?" she pressed. "You don't seem to be dismissive of it, even though she died."

He lifted his hands, trying to find a way to express his thoughts. "I didn't expect a cure, and I don't think she did either. And I have my own health issues that are making me think about alternative methods lately." He had, in fact, spent half his afternoon searching the internet for some sort of blood pressure treatment. Something that a hospital couldn't offer.

Her lips curved in a soft smile. "An open mind. I like that."

"Yeah," he said slowly. "You know, I'm beginning to think the universe does work in mysterious ways." Because right here, right in front of him might be the answer to his prayers. But just in case he was wrong, he tried to think logically about it. He started tallying up facts in his brain.

His blood pressure was out of control. So out of control, he might have to quit his job.

He'd exhausted all the options that modern medicine could offer.

She was a doctor, but was serious about alternative methods and sounded like she took a scientific approach.

He needed to find a cure. Maybe she had the answer.

"So," he said, feigning casualness, "find any therapies that work?"

She nodded, the most confident movement she'd made during the entire discussion. "I think so, yes."

"Okay then," he said, coming to a quick decision. "I'm game. Let's do it."

She blinked, obviously not following him. He didn't blame her. It's not like he had explained where his brain had taken him.

He smiled. "You're a former doctor doing scientific research into energy healing."

She nodded.

"Well, I'm a patient who's looking for some nonstandard treatments. For high blood pressure. Really high blood pressure."

She gaped at him. "What?"

"I want to hire you, Amber. For the magical mystery tour of energy healing. I'll do whatever you want, however you want, so long as I don't have to quit my job to do it."

6

AMBER STARED AT the man who had just given her the two top orgasms of her life. "You want me to be your *doctor?*"

"Yes," he said firmly, as if that made all the sense in the world.

"Do you know how completely unethical that is? I mean, we just… You…" She couldn't even put into words what they had done except that it had been incredible. The last thing she wanted was to suddenly step into a *professional* relationship with him.

He just waved away her concerns with a mild shrug. "Well, you just said you're a researcher now, not really a doctor."

"That doesn't mean—"

"And I'm not asking for traditional medical science, obviously. Been there, done that, and it's not working. I want you to do the other stuff. Acupuncture, voodoo, mystical whatever." He spread his arms wide. "Experiment on me. Just so long as I can keep my job."

She sighed. She hadn't thought of him as a quick fix kind of guy. From what she'd heard and seen of him so far, he made quick decisions, but that was because he was a quick thinker. Not because he was searching for a short cut.

"I'm sure your doctor discussed with you all the other options for lowering your blood pressure. Diet, exercise—"

"Yeah. I'm doing it. Not helping."

"Medications."

He ran through the litany of meds he'd already tried. She leaned forward.

"Just how high is your blood pressure?"

He reached into his jacket pocket and pulled out a little card where he had recorded all his readings for the last five months. Her eyebrows shot up. Yes, he certainly did have a problem. "How long has it been like this?"

"Climbing steadily since my teens. You're looking at my stable point for the last year and half."

"And you've been on—"

"Every hypertension medication known to mankind."

She passed back his card while trying to keep her expression neutral. From what he described, he certainly needed something. If modern medicine wasn't helping him, then he had to look elsewhere. She knew exactly what she'd recommend for him, but it was drastic and not even remotely guaranteed.

"So?" he pressed. "Will you do it? Will you help me?"

She shook her head. "I can't be your doctor. I won't. We're…" She didn't want to say they were in a relationship, because they weren't. But they certainly weren't strangers, either. "There are some lines I won't cross."

He sighed. "Fair enough. But how about advice? You give advice to friends, right? And after this, I'd really like to call you a friend."

She cautiously nodded. Yes, she could see him as a friend.

"Okay then, *friend,* what would you recommend for me?"

She bit her lip and pulled out the most drastic course of

action she could think of in the hopes that he would compromise and do at least some of the items on her list. "As a friend, I would tell you that I think you should go on a raw-food diet, start meditating and hire someone to do energy sessions on you. And, of course, take a long vacation—right now—to really examine your life. Something's out of whack and you won't know what it is until you stop completely and listen."

To his credit, he didn't even blink. But he did have a question. "Listen to what? Meditation tapes like mantras and stuff?"

She shook her head. "To your body. To your soul. To what you really want to have in your life and what needs to just disappear."

He shrugged. "That's easy. My body likes red meat, my job and you. And not necessarily in that order."

She laughed because he was being absolutely serious and kind of sweet at the same time. "As your friend, I recommend you do a two-week retreat. Raw food, yoga, meditation and absolutely no electronics whatsoever."

He frowned. "How is that different from quitting my job?"

"How is *dying* from a heart attack different from quitting your job?"

He huffed and closed his eyes. "You sound just like my doctor."

She stepped forward because he really did have a problem. He was pretending to have a flippant attitude, but she could see the fear in his eyes. The man was up against a wall, and he knew it. So she touched his cheek. And then, because she couldn't resist, she pressed her mouth to his. A moment later, his arm had snaked around her waist and he was hauling her closer. Bam, her blood started sizzling in her veins.

"I hear lots of sex is good for hypertension," he said.

She might have said something snarky in response.

Something about men, and sex being their answer to all of life's problems. But he didn't give her time and before long, she'd lost the thread of her thoughts beneath the amazing skill of his tongue.

Then the ceiling fell in on them.

Perhaps that was fortunate, though, because nothing short of a ceiling access panel falling on their heads would have gotten their attention. As it was, Amber was tempted to just keep going. But that was because Roger took the worst of the impact.

"Ow! What the—"

"Sorry! Sorry about that!" came a voice from above.

Amber looked up to see a man in coveralls poking his head through the top of the elevator. Roger rubbed his head and glared at the newcomer.

"A little warning next time would be nice," he groused. Then he frowned. "And why aren't you at your bachelor party?"

Ah! thought Amber. This was Sam Finn, CEO of RFE. The genius inventor and Roger's best friend. And obviously the man who was about to get married.

"Someone had to rescue you. Might as well be me."

"You could have texted me that there was an access panel up there. Geez, we would have climbed out on our own."

Sam just laughed. "I did, buddy. Apparently, you were too busy doing something else to look at your phone."

Amber flushed at that. Had they really been so involved that they hadn't even noticed their rescue? She didn't need to answer the question. Obviously, they had been.

Sam leaped down into the elevator. Clearly, the man had done this before. He went immediately to the panel and popped it open, using some sort of handheld device to diagnose the problem. "I'm Sam, by the way," he said over his shoulder.

"I'm Roger's boss, best friend and designated rescuer this week."

"And I'm yours every damn day of the week," Roger shot back.

Amber laughed. She could tell from the byplay that they were friends of long standing. They might poke at each other, but clearly the bond between them ran deep.

"I'm Amber," she said warmly. "And I'm Roger's friend. Therefore, as his friend, I am breeching no confidentiality at all when I tell you that he needs to take a vacation. *Now.* For his health. Like starting yesterday and for a couple of weeks at least."

Roger reacted exactly as she expected: with anger and a flash of betrayal in his eyes. She was sorry for that. Truly sorry. But for his own good, Roger needed his friends to force him to take that long break.

Meanwhile, Sam twisted to look at his friend. "Is that true?"

Roger huffed. "Look, we're going to have to fly out next month to the Mandolin Clinic—"

Sam straightened with a look of alarm.

"For business!" Roger scrambled to say. "There's a doctor there who's open to working with us on some products. There are some exciting possibilities."

Sam ignored him, his expression narrowing. "This about your blood pressure?"

Roger grimaced. "I'll take a vacation right after the meeting."

Sam nodded slowly. "What about the convention next month?"

Roger frowned. "Oh, yeah. It'll have to be after that. There's a lot to prepare—"

"And then there's the audit. Not a big deal, but you usually—"

"Yeah," Roger groaned. "I want to be here for that."

Sam rubbed his chin. Then he looked directly at Amber. "How serious is his condition?"

Amber shrugged. "As you can see, he looks and feels fine. But I believe he needs to get control of it now."

Sam glanced at his friend. "By way of a vacation? Health spa or something, right?"

Roger shifted so he was standing between the two of them. "I'll take a vacation. Soon. I swear."

Sam shook his head. "No, you'll take one now or you're fired. We can handle things without you for a while."

"You can't even keep the elevator running!"

Sam shot his friend a look as he pressed a button. Right on cue, the elevator hummed to life. A moment later, the doors opened on the ground floor. Roger and Amber stepped out while Sam continued to tap keys on his pad. Roger turned back to look at his friend, a flush of desperation in his face.

"Sam, look, I know you care, but this vacation thing isn't the real—"

"Hey, Roger," interrupted Sam. "Thanks for the bachelor party. It was really great, and the guys are still out there having the kind of time an engaged man shouldn't enjoy."

"Sam—"

"You're a great best man. Now, if I see you again in the next two weeks, you're fired. No joke, man, you know I'm serious. Do what you need to do to get healthy."

"I can't just disappear, Sam. I need to—"

Sam wasn't listening. He waved pleasantly to Amber. "Nice meeting you." Then he pushed a button and the elevator doors started closing.

Roger leaped forward, but it was too late. The metal doors shut tight. "Sam!" he bellowed. Then he slammed his briefcase against the elevator doors. "Sam, you arrogant bastard!"

No response. Not that he seemed to expect one. Instead, he

just stood there, fuming silently. Amber thought about sneaking away. Maybe she could slip into the shadows before he remembered she was there. But she nixed the thought almost immediately. After all, she was the one who had told his friend and boss about the problem. It was only fair that she stand here and take the consequences. Besides, given the state of his blood pressure, he might well be about to have a coronary.

"Go ahead," she said. "Kick it. Scream a bit. Don't hold all that fury inside."

He spun around to glare at her. "You had to tell him."

"I'm not your doctor," she said firmly. "And as your friend, I'm worried about your health."

"Are you worried about whether or not I'm going to strangle you?"

She smiled because she detected a hint of humor beneath his words. "No," she answered truthfully. "I'm worried you're going to stroke out right now before we can get you feeling better."

"I. Feel. Fine!"

She nodded, but didn't back down despite the fury on his face. "Okay, I'll make you a deal. And it's one I can't check on my own, so I'm trusting in your honesty."

He arched a brow. He was listening.

"I'm willing to go right back upstairs now and tell Sam I was wrong. That you've got everything completely under control and that we can trust your judgment on your health."

"Really?" he drawled, suspicion in every syllable.

"Yeah. Provided you can do one thing."

He waited in silence.

"I want you to close your eyes, breathe deeply and not think of anything at all for one minute. Just listen. To your breath, to the sounds in the garage, to how your body feels. Just listen. Not a single word or thought attached to it."

He frowned. "That's all?"

"Yup. That's it. Frankly, I'll be surprised if you last more than three seconds."

"Ha. I used to do this with my mother." He dropped his briefcase, folding his arms across his chest, then leaned back against the garage wall. "Bring it on, baby," he snapped.

"Not a single thought."

"Just listening. I got it." He arched a brow at her. "It's not like I haven't done this meditation crap before."

She smiled. Now she was getting down to the real Roger. A half hour ago, he wouldn't have dismissed her beliefs with words like "meditation crap." But right now he was really ticked off, and so his true thoughts were shining through. She counted that as progress, so she held out her hand in the friendliest gesture she could make.

"I'll need to use your watch. I don't have one."

He frowned. "You don't have a watch?"

"Not since I left Mandolin."

He gave her a disbelieving look as he whipped off his tasteful digital watch and passed it to her. She took it and waited as he composed himself.

"Ready?" she asked.

"Yes," he returned, his voice deep and even. That surprised her. Obviously, he really had done some meditation on his own. She could already see how his shoulders dropped and his breathing began to even out.

"Go."

She started the timer on his watch. The seconds started to tick by. As long as he was trying to meditate, she should do the same, becoming as present as possible in the current moment. Her vision blurred out slightly, and like him, her breath steadied. She heard the sounds from the street outside, but then pulled her focus deeper. She listened to the draw of air in her lungs and heard the pulse of blood in her right ear, an annoying symptom she had yet to resolve. With her next exhale, she consciously released the judgment and frustration she held in that thought. And then she released the thought about releasing her thoughts.

Barely two seconds later, she began to wonder how Roger was doing. Without willing it, her gaze snapped to him. His eyes were closed, his breath steady. Perhaps she had misjudged him. Perhaps he did know how to release his stress in a silent meditation.... Perhaps he was doing way better than she was because, frankly, she'd been thinking this whole time.

She pulled her attention back to her own silence, refocusing on *not* thinking. She managed it for seven seconds before she started wondering about Roger again. His breath was a little louder now, but in the silence of the garage, she heard it like an alarm.

Her gaze lifted to his and she saw him staring at her, his expression unreadable. A glance back at his watch told her it had only been thirty-four seconds.

"What are you thinking about?" she asked.

He glanced down at himself before back up at her. "You can't guess?"

It took a moment for her to understand, and then her gaze dropped to his groin. Well, okay then. He had a rather impressive erection going.

She stifled a laugh. "As a doctor, I can state with confidence that hypertension has not adversely impacted your sexual responses."

"Ya think?"

She didn't even try to stop her snort at that. Then she sobered. "I take it I win the bet. You were thinking, weren't you? Not just...um...experiencing the physical changes, right?"

"Thinking, visualizing, just about everything a man can do without actually doing."

She didn't know what to say to that. Unfortunately, her body had all sorts of ideas and suggestions, all of which flashed in her mind's eye. Apparently, he wasn't the only one who could visualize in detail.

"So," he said in a flat tone. "What now?"

She blinked. "Um, I guess I recommend some holistic retreats. They can be kinda pricey, but you're—"

"No need. I already have a retreat location in mind."

She frowned. "You do?"

"Yeah. Your place. Or mine, I suppose."

Okay, so her body was all kinds of good with that idea. But her mind slammed the door shut. "Roger, you need to take this seriously. Sex isn't—"

"I *am* taking this seriously. You have no idea how seriously. But since you're the *friend* who spilled the beans to my boss, you're the friend who's going to help me fix this particular problem."

She huffed and threw up her hands. "This isn't an instant cure. It's not just drink some tea, stab yourself with some acupuncture needles and you're fine. This is serious work, and it's a life choice."

He picked up his briefcase and readjusted his jacket. "Okay. Life choice. I *choose* you to help me fix this."

"But—"

"Amber, please. I'm out of ideas here and rapidly running out of time. Thirteen different medications, one drug study and relatives up the wazoo who died from heart attacks. You think I don't know that I'm in trouble? I do. I have for a long time. I just don't know what to do about it!" He took a deep breath. "So, please. Will you help me?"

It was the vulnerability in his eyes that decided her. His face was rather still, kept rigidly under control, she suspected. But his eyes were pleading, and there was that slight hitch in his tone. He was a lot more desperate than he seemed.

But the big question here was whether she could help him, give him the advice he wanted without jumping him at every opportunity. He wasn't the only one humming with desire right now. She'd just had two of the best orgasms of her life, and she was beyond ready to do it again. Her skin was flushed, her nipples tight and her legs were weak. This was a whole new level of attraction for her, and yet here he was asking her to give him medical advice. It just didn't seem to compute. And yet, no way could she turn him away. Not before, when he'd pushed her up against the elevator wall, and not now.

"My place," she finally said. "I'll fix you dinner."

7

ROGER FOLLOWED Amber home, driving behind her little Miata to what was once a warehouse district but was now converted crap. Housing crap where the poor, the struggling and the deluded lived. He could hardly believe it when she parked and got out of her car as if she were safe. He pulled in behind her, parking right in front of a fire hydrant. He'd risk the ticket rather than let her walk alone on the real-life set of *Rent*.

"Amber, wait up!" He was out of his car in a second, wondering if this was the last he'd see of his Infinity M in this neighborhood. "You seriously live here?"

Her lips quirked, or at least he thought they did. It was hard to see in the sparse city light. "I seriously do," she answered. Then she leaned down and touched the shoulder of a homeless guy set up in a building doorway. "Hello, Tammy. How's that cough today?"

"Better, Doc. Much—" Hack, hack, *sneeze*. "Wow, that was a big one, Doc. You must be getting more powerful!"

Roger barely resisted jumping away. Okay, so the homeless guy was actually a woman who was now wiping her nose with her sleeve. Amber just smiled and patted the woman's shoulder. "Get some fresh fruit, Tammy. Salad would be even better."

"Can't afford it," the woman said as she held out her hand to Roger. "But if your young man would help…"

Amber chuckled and moved away. She didn't even wait for Roger to dig a five out of his wallet. He normally would have walked on past, but he couldn't just leave an old woman sitting in the street. Not one that he'd spoken to. But he worried that he was opening himself up to being harassed by every homeless person in a five-mile radius.

"Oh, thank you. You're a kind man…" murmured Tammy. Up ahead, Amber stopped walking long enough to turn around with her hands planted on her hips.

"You better share that, Tammy. Buy some fruit!"

"Rum's made from fruit, right?"

Amber just shook her head, but she did gesture to Roger's car. "And keep his car safe, will ya? As thanks for the cash?"

Tammy didn't answer. Just crossed her arms and huffed as she leaned back against the wall. Roger caught up to Amber and leaned close.

"Will she do it?"

Amber just shrugged. "Dunno. Depends on her mood." Then she opened the door of a converted apartment building and started inside. He followed, climbing three flights of stairs before she finally stopped at a heavy iron sliding door. "Home, sweet home," she quipped as she unlocked it and hauled it open.

He followed inside, not knowing what to think. She was still dressed in her suit and heels, though her hair was now freely flowing down her shoulders. She looked expensive and soft at the same time, just the right combination for his libido. Putting her in this environment just messed with his head. It didn't fit, but while he got more uncomfortable, she seemed to relax, settling into a quiet confidence that startled him.

The Power Queen who had hit his office an hour ago was confident in the way of all women who demanded respect. She'd exuded dominance in every move, every breath. But here, in this neighborhood, she'd completely abandoned that persona. What he saw now was a woman at ease with who and what she was.

It was an odd impression, especially since they'd done no more than walk a city block together, but he couldn't shake it. And now, as he entered her apartment, the feeling got stronger. It was a huge, open place furnished with almost nothing. A scarred desk teetered in the corner, propped up under one leg by a stack of books. A large metal cabinet lay right next to it, closed by a massive padlock. A couch that must have been purchased at a garage sale dominated the center. And through a side door, he saw a bedroom complete with crates that served as holders for her clothes and a large futon bed. That, plus a couple of large plants, was the extent of her decor.

And yet, he felt a sense of peace when he walked in the door. A quiet that made him breathe deeply the minute he crossed the threshold. And he saw an echoing movement in her. She lifted her chin, smiled at one of the plants and released a slow happy exhale.

"You love it here," he said.

She looked at him. "It's my home." She spread her arms wide. "My *space*." And there was a lot of that here: empty space. Yet it worked for her. And it apparently worked for him, too, because he found himself smiling at her Spartan existence.

"I like it," he said with a bit of shock.

"Have a seat. I'm going to change."

She disappeared into her bedroom as he stripped out of his suit jacket and then settled on her couch. But as he sat there, he began to fidget. She didn't have any real music to speak of. No TV, no coffee table books, no coffee table even. No distractions of any sort, it seemed. And in the silence, he decided he needed to check his email.

Flipping open his BlackBerry, he thumbed through his messages until he saw that nothing exciting had happened in the twenty minutes since he'd left the office. No big surprise there. It was late on a Friday night, after all. But he still flipped through his mail searching for something to do.

"Checking in at work?" she asked as she came out from her bedroom. She was wearing a pair of yoga pants and a tight tank. Her hair was no longer softly waving about her face and shoulders, but tied back in a hasty ponytail. And as she walked, he saw that she'd abandoned her boots in favor of bare feet that didn't even sport nail polish.

He found himself grinning at her. She looked awesome in a completely different way. In fact, if he hadn't seen her step into her bedroom, he might have thought she was two completely different people. Sisters, perhaps. And this was the younger, wilder, happier one.

"You are a woman of many surprises," he said softly.

She laughed, the sound free and breezy. "No. Just one surprise. This is Amber," she said as she went into the kitchen and wet a washcloth. A minute later, she was wiping the makeup off her face, not that there'd been a lot in the first place. When she turned back to him, her skin was pink and fresh. "The woman you met before was Dr. Smithson, and she doesn't really exist anymore. Unless, of course, she's bent on catching the eye of the hot robotics executive."

"Well, I was definitely caught," he drawled. "But I gotta say, I really like Amber."

"And I'd really like your BlackBerry." She crossed to him, her hand outstretched.

"What?"

"Give it up, Roger."

He passed it to her, mostly because he was pretty sure he could get it back if he wanted. He was wrong. She crossed to the large metal cabinet, undid the padlock and dropped the cell into a plastic basket inside.

"Wait a minute…" he said, but she shook her head and firmly relocked the door.

"You're officially unplugged. No iPod, no cell phones, no distractions while you're in this place. Doc Crystal's rules. I live in a quiet space."

"As a rule, electronics aren't that noisy. I'll even turn off the ringer."

She smiled as she shook her head, her ponytail bobbing attractively about her shoulders. "Quiet isn't about just sound, Roger. It's about a quiet soul. You can't hear your soul while you're checking email."

He looked at her without speaking. It's not that he objected to what she said, only that she looked so normal as she said it. Her words were supposed to come out of the mouths of sixties hippies or evangelists who wanted him to plug into God. But it was just her, looking calm and sane and yet telling him to listen to his soul.

He gestured out the iron-grated window. "You say that to the homeless people, too? To listen to their souls?"

"Absolutely. And I make them give up their iPods, too."

He leaned back on the couch. "They have iPods?"

She shrugged. "You'd be surprised what they come in here with." Then she went back into the kitchen and popped open an old refrigerator. "I believe I promised you dinner."

He moved to her kitchen, leaning up against the breakfast bar that didn't have any stools. "You know what? I've got a better idea. How about I take you out to dinner? You pick the restaurant. How about Antonio's downtown? I love Italian. Or I just found this great sushi place. We could—"

"Nope." Just that. A flat, no-nonsense denial.

"Not a sushi fan."

"I love sushi. One of the things I miss."

"Perfect. Then—"

"Nope." She pulled out two massive serving bowls from a cabinet, then started dropping big fistfuls of spinach leaves into them.

"Um, Amber? That's a lot of spinach there."

She glanced up at him, barely pausing as she started dropping in cherry tomatoes. "You're a big guy," she said.

Well, he had asked her to help with his blood pressure. Salad was likely to be part of the menu for some time to come. "Can I help with the cooking? I know a ton of great lean chicken recipes."

She smiled as she started dropping shriveled blueberries into the huge bowls. "That's sweet."

He pushed away from the breakfast bar. "So where are your pans?"

"It's sweet but completely unneeded. Relax. Kick back on the couch if you like."

He shook his head. "I like it right here watching you work." And he did. Her movements were almost breezy as she shook slivered almonds onto the salad. Then came a few mandarin orange pieces from a jar and she was pushing the bowl at him.

"Oh!" She spun around. "You probably want something to drink, too!" A minute later, she pushed a tall glass of filtered water toward him. Then she brandished two forks, one for each of them, and gave him a big grin. *"Bon appétit!"*

He arched a brow at her. "It looks great," he said. "If a bit huge."

She flashed him a grin. "Well, as I said, you're a big guy. I figured you'd want a lot."

"This is all that's for dinner, isn't it? No chicken, no wine, not even any low-fat tasteless fish, huh?"

She set down her fork, her expression shifting to what had to be her authoritative doctor face. He bristled immediately, but was careful to keep his reaction hidden.

"You asked me to help you control your blood pressure. You begged me to do some New Age mumbo jumbo on you. You've had it with standard medicine and now you're looking to the weird."

"All true," he admitted.

"Well, here it is, Roger. My prescription, so to speak, is a daily regimen of meditation—"

"Yeah, that's what I expected—"

"And live food only."

He paused a moment, trying to understand her words. Wasn't all food live? Or at least had been. Or… "What?"

"Food that has not been cooked, processed or damaged in any way. It's got the highest energy vibration and is easiest on your system. Plus, it aids in detoxification and has a host of beneficial effects that are too numerous to count."

He blinked. "Living food. As in salad."

"As in fruits, vegetables and nuts." She reached beneath the counter and pulled out two bowls, one of apples and another smaller one of raw peanuts. Then she looked at him, one brow arched in challenge.

And that's when he figured it out. He'd forced her into this. Not as in a gun to her head, but there'd been some pressure, some manipulation. He was desperate for a solution, so he'd pushed her to help him. So, in reaction, she was making her "prescription" as hideous as possible, expecting him to turn tail and run.

But he had her number. No person could live like that. Even Tibetan monks ate rice and cheese. He dropped his chin on his palm as he looked at her. "And how long am I supposed to be on this diet?"

"Ideally? The rest of your life."

He snorted at that. He couldn't help himself. "Salad. For the rest of my life."

"Or until you get control of your blood pressure. But I gotta tell you, I've been raw for seventeen months now, and I'm not going back."

He laughed, really laughed at that. No way was she really committed to a lifetime of eating only rabbit food. She forgot that he'd been up close and personal with her body. He knew the muscles that supported her frame. He'd felt the grip in her legs and the power in her orgasm. To get muscles like that, she had to have more protein in her diet than what she could get from a few raw peanuts.

She was making all this up. Just yanking his chain so he'd turn and leave. But he had no interest in leaving. Not yet, at least. He didn't stop to examine his thoughts too deeply. He just knew that he was up for whatever challenge she threw at him—so long as she matched him bite for unappetizing bite.

"Fine," he said. "All raw. So you got a piece of cheese somewhere?"

She shook her head. "No dairy. Just trust me on this. It causes more problems than it solves. And before you ask, no coffee either."

"I went decaf a year ago."

She nodded. "Good. That'll make it easier on you."

He smiled slowly at her. "I don't even eat chocolate."

"Really? Wow. That's just crazy."

He laughed at that because she meant him to. And because it was funny that she would draw the line at giving up chocolate. Then he sobered, trying to impress on her the truth of his next words.

"Amber, I'm sorry I manipulated you into helping me."

"You didn't—"

He held up his hand. "I did, and I'm sorry. And I really am serious about addressing the hypertension."

"Very good."

"So can we dispense with the game playing?" he asked. "I'll do the meditation. I'll take supplements. I'll even cover my body with crystals while sniffing peppermint. Whatever. But let's do this for real."

Her expression matched his for seriousness as she stroked one long finger down his cheek. "I'm not playing games, Roger. Raw food. For real. Or you can go home now with my best prayers for you."

"And nothing else. I'd never see you again."

She bit her lip, obviously conflicted. "You asked for my friendly advice. You're getting it. As for not seeing you again…" she shook her head "…I don't know. I haven't processed the, um, the other yet."

Neither had he. So he went back to the advice he'd forced her to give him. "So, raw food. No dairy. Just…"

"Living food," she said with a nod. "There's no halfway right now. Maybe not ever."

He zeroed in on the wiggle room in her statement. "You mean I can go back to a normal healthy diet once my blood pressure drops?"

She brandished her fork. "The definition of healthy diet is rather flexible, don't you think? Changes drastically depending on who you ask."

He had no argument to that, just the certainty that he had run out of all the standard options. And he already did the healthy diet and exercise. It wasn't like she was suggesting he inject some bizarre concoction into his veins. Hell, she wasn't asking him to do anything beyond eating salad and contemplating his navel for a while. In terms of drasticness, it wasn't all that bad. And it was way better than quitting his job, which was what everyone else had told him to do.

"Fine," he said, giving in with as much grace as he could muster. "Where's the salad dressing?"

"Oh," she said, biting her lip. "I haven't made any up. I never use it. Here. Try this." She grabbed a rather sad-looking lemon and sliced it in half before squeezing it over his bowl of leaves.

Great. Just great. He forced himself to smile as he dug in. This cure better work damn fast or he was thinking going die from the frustration of *not* eating a steak. Hell, forget red meat. At this point, he was thinking longingly of a lean piece of chicken breast. And then she added one more piece of misery to the pot.

"After dinner, we'll do a little yoga to relax and then start meditating."

8

It wasn't until Roger stripped out of his clothes that Amber realized the depth of her mistake. So far he'd accepted her decrees with less grumbling than she had done two years ago when she decided to completely change her life. He'd eaten his salad and managed to pretend he liked it. It was really kind of endearing the way he kept saying that it was good to have greens stripped down to their natural flavors. She wondered how many salads it would take before the "natural flavors" started losing their appeal.

They'd talked casually during their meal, chatting about her move to Chicago, about the favorite parts of his job and, best of all, his favorite Broadway shows. There was a time when she'd made a point of seeing the most recent productions, and it was wonderful to discuss the pros and cons of stage versus screen or book. It's not like she had a lot of that kind of talk with Tammy or her other neighbors.

But then as the light began to dim, she declared it was time for yoga. After all, that was her usual routine. She saw no reason for it to be different than any other night. She'd often shared her evening practice with one or more of her neighbors.

But tonight she wasn't stretching with Sandy, the single

mother down the hall. It wasn't even like the slow practice she sometimes did with Miller, the emaciated alcoholic who was struggling against his addiction. Tonight, she'd be working out with Roger—who didn't have a change of clothes. Ripped, muscular and very macho Roger, who said he could do yoga just fine in his boxers. After all, she'd already seen all the important parts of his body. By comparison, this was almost sedate.

Except now he stood before her, completely naked except for a pair of silk boxers covered in tiny robots playing basketball, and there wasn't any part of his body that she could look at without blushing. Not the corded expanse of his chest. Not the bulky muscles of his thighs. Not even the tiny little orange basketballs that danced over his boxers. Nope. In fact, every single inch of his glorious body brought her skin to heated, blushing, sensuous life. And all he'd done was disrobe in front of her.

God, she was depraved. She'd gone nearly two years without sex. She'd been so chaste she'd practically regrown her virginity. Then one single elevator mishap later, and she'd become a sex addict.

"So now what?" Roger asked, looking a little awkward standing before her in his underwear. He didn't cover himself with his hands or do anything else obviously nervous. He just stood before her, his arms loose by his sides, as he rose up onto the balls of his feet then rocked back down. He looked like an animal thinking about attacking something. And, depraved woman that she was, she wanted him to leap on her.

"It's—" Her voice came out on a squeak, so she had to clear her throat and try again. "Couples yoga is really simple. Just face me and mimic my actions. I'll walk you through anything hard."

He arched a brow at her, but didn't comment. He'd already told her that he'd never done yoga before, but was ready to try.

His whole attitude had been slightly dismissive. After all, he was athletic. How difficult could some stretching be?

She'd smirked in response, and the game was on. Her goal this evening was to make him sweat. Just a little. Just enough to bring a sheen to his glorious chest and a gasp of relief when they finally stopped. She just hadn't counted on how good he looked standing facing her.

"Are we going to start soon?" he asked. "Or is this part of it? Am I supposed to be meditating or something?"

She flushed. "Um, sorry. I was just thinking."

His smirk told her he knew exactly what she'd been thinking, and that he was more than ready to ditch the yoga in favor of the "couple" part of the practice. Part of her heartily agreed. But what she said was a very stern, "Try to stop thinking. Just center yourself in your body."

He blinked. "I have no idea what that's supposed to mean."

"Stop thinking about sex," she returned.

"Then you need to change into a parka."

Zing. She hadn't even realized her nipples had tightened, but at his words, she became very aware of every horny inch of her breasts and groin. Lord, this was *not* going to work. But she had to try it anyway.

"Inhale as you raise your arms up to the sky," she intoned, fitting words to action. He mimicked her, and she couldn't help but watch the way his chest expanded and his pectoral muscles seemed to dance as he raised his arms. Shadows were such amazing things, she thought. They flicked in and out of existence according to the shift and slide of his body.

"Exhale and bend over. Try to keep your legs straight without locking them."

She bent over, stretching her buttocks high as was the pose. Of course, that reminded her of when she'd done exactly this in the elevator and the way he had pushed right in. She gasped in memory, her concentration shot. She barely managed to say the next words.

"Touch your fingertips down, then arch your head up and back into monkey pose."

She demonstrated, feeling the pull in her hamstrings, the arch in her back and the general lengthening in her spine. Until she realized that she had misjudged the distance between them. As he lifted his face, they were barely two inches apart. Their foreheads nearly collided, but that was nothing compared to the way their gazes locked and held.

She watched his nostrils flare, felt heat lick her skin, and her legs went weak with hunger.

"We need to be in our bodies."

"I'm not having an out-of-body experience," he drawled. "You?"

"Not what I meant," she returned rather curtly. Then she moderated her tone. It wasn't his fault that she couldn't keep her mind out of the gutter. "Don't think of anything but your body. Just feel the stretch of muscles, the air filling your lungs—"

"The way my dick is so hard this position is painful."

She blinked. "Oh! Sorry." Her cheeks felt like they were on fire from her blush. "Um, right. Release your head and neck, then roll back up to vertical. Try and let your vertebrae click into place one by one."

She fitted words to action, but her mind was on his words and the way her body was liquid with desire. She'd wanted to see him sweat, but she was the one who was wet. And in these light gray yoga pants, it wouldn't be long until he knew it, too.

Then they were standing again, facing each other. She couldn't stop herself from seeing his erection. It was huge and right there in front of her. In fact, they were so close together her mind immediately conjured at least seven poses that would force her to touch it. And just like that she started guiding him into one of them. It wasn't a conscious decision. It just happened. At least that's what she told herself.

"Step your right foot forward and slowly extend into a lunge."

To show him, she lengthened herself into a lunge. She stepped unerringly to the place she wanted, her knee level with his hips and their bodies much too close. Then his step took them to the point of nearly touching.

"Now stay in your lunge and lift your left hip, opening up to face me more."

She did as she said, squaring her hips and torso toward him. She knew her nipples were tight, felt as if her whole body was a guitar wire humming with life. She told herself she was simply opening up to the energy that infused all things, herself included. But the truth was that her body and blood were humming with lust. Unfortunately, things weren't going as well for Roger.

This wasn't a pose he could do easily. The lunge was no problem, though he hadn't stepped far enough. It was the opening of his hips that would be difficult for any man. Add to that the erection that stretched hard against his boxers, and he was probably dying.

"You're doing fine," she said as she stroked a hand along his back leg. "Can you slide your front foot forward a bit more?"

He tried, but his foot caught on her rug. In the end, he had to hop it forward, bouncing awkwardly. She kept her hand on his leg, feeling the tremble in this thigh, and her other went to his chest to steady him. And then he stilled, his right knee extended before him.

"Now," she said as she stroked up along his back leg, "shift this hip up and open."

He narrowed his eyes in a frown. "Open my hip?"

She nodded and put her hands on his hips, slowly exerting pressure on the top hip while pulling the bottom toward her. He couldn't go far. He wasn't flexible enough in that direction. And then it didn't matter because his heel slid as he tried to adjust. Her grip wasn't meant to restrain him, just to encourage, so as he moved, she did, too. And a second later, she was stroking his penis instead of his hips.

Oops. And double oops because she didn't stop the long caress.

"I think I'm beginning to like yoga," he drawled, his voice a low rumble.

She let go of him in a second, her heart beating in her throat. "That's not yoga, and you know it."

"I'm not complaining," he said, but she shook her head and scooted backward. Not away from him, but farther up his body toward his chest. She needed to be close enough to touch him, to help him find the positions. But she didn't need to be quite so far down his body.

"Okay," she said breathlessly, as she found her position. "Can you lengthen your torso—still facing me—along your bent leg? Think of yourself as stretching your elbow to your bent knee."

"You're kidding, right?"

"Nope." Then she did it. Or as much of the pose as she could manage. And here's where she realized how very, very depraved she was. She was guiding him through a real pose, one she did every day. But never before had she managed to put her face right next to anyone's crotch. Never before had she inhaled deeply or shifted her hands to slip down her partner's boxers. Two seconds later, she had him in her mouth.

"Oh, Jesus," he breathed, his body frozen. Probably in shock. Her own back leg gave out and she dropped to one knee before him. But he was still in his lunge, and his shorts were stretched taut, preventing her from getting the full length of him.

Then his back leg gave out as well. It didn't go quickly, in a sudden jerk, but in an excruciatingly slow shift of tension until he, too, was down on one knee. And now, her hands could tug his boxers to below his buttocks.

"Amber," he breathed, his hands on her shoulders. She felt his bottom tighten as she tongued him. Around and along his length. Loving the way he shuddered beneath her ministrations. "Amber!"

He pulled her off him. Not hard and certainly not fast. And when she looked up into his eyes, she saw a sparkle of humor there that felt odd. Or it did until he spoke.

"You said to mirror your movements exactly." Then he put his hands on her pants and pushed them down over her bottom. She gasped in surprise as he used his larger weight to topple her backward. She was already down on one knee, so she didn't have far to go. He managed—somehow—to get a hand behind her head so she didn't bang it. And then, the minute she was on the floor, he was back to her knees, pulling her pants down off her feet.

She should have stopped him. This was not at all what she'd meant by relaxing yoga. But her blood was already simmering, she'd already tasted him. And the desire to feel him surging beneath her again made her give up any pretense of exercise. Especially as his lips found the inside of her thighs.

"Roger," she said, her voice unnaturally low. "You don't have to…" He lifted her knee and began licking his way up. Then he stopped to shoot her a pretend serious look.

"You said to mirror your every move. Believe me, I intend to."

She swallowed. What he was doing was making her belly quiver and her blood heat to boiling. "Then," she said, "I suppose I ought to show you what you should do next."

She rolled to her side and found what she wanted. He was thick and hard and right before her eyes. She grasped him with her hand and rolled her thumb across the top, spreading the bead of moisture there. And then she arched in desire as she felt his thumb do the same to her. He pressed between her folds to slide up and around her clit. Her body arched at the exquisite feel. She wanted him to do that again. She wanted…

She rolled her thumb up and around. So did he. It was delicious and kind of kinky, feeling this echo to whatever she did to him.

She stroked him all the way down to his balls, gripping and squeezing him just enough to hear him hiss. He slid his thumb down between her folds, then thrust inside her. Not quite an identical gesture but the sensations were beyond thrilling. But she was getting impatient, her body already anxious for more. So she went ahead and did what they both wanted.

She took him in her mouth. She gripped his base and sucked him in. And he, in turn, put his lips to her clit and began to tease. Tongue swirl, then suction, then a rapid flick. She experienced all of that in wild chaotic succession, over and over again. She lost track of what she was doing to him. It was too much and yet not enough.

She felt his hips buck and his buttocks tighten. Meanwhile, her back was arching, her body trembling. She couldn't catch her breath. Just as she was pulling back to gasp for air, he abruptly pulled himself away. Then he pressed her hip backward until she was flat on her back. She would have protested. She intended to. But with the better angle, he began to do amazing things to her.

Within moments she was pumping her groin against him. A flick, a swirl and then he sucked. Hard. She cried out as the wave hit her, but he was pinning her down, his tongue still doing things to her while she thrashed beneath him. Wave after wave crashed through her body. Oh, God, she couldn't take it and...

Oh, yes! She cried out. She thrashed and she bucked, and finally, she bucked him off. And then she was floating in wave after wave of pleasure. Slowly catching her breath. Slowly, smiling.

Finally, she could lean down toward him and grab him by the ears. Then she said two words directly to his face.

"Condom. Now!"

9

HE EXPLODED INTO HER. He didn't think he could do it again, and yet here he was, erupting like a teenage boy. At least they'd made it to her bed this time. After they'd finished the best damn yoga practice he'd ever imagined, they'd stumbled to her futon. She'd spooned back against him, murmuring something about closing her eyes for just a minute. But at that moment, he'd realized how very wonderful she smelled. No perfume, no special herbal scent, just her and the scent was surprisingly sweet. So he'd nuzzled closer to her. And once that close, he had to taste her neck because it was right there. Then his hands naturally found her breasts because they were the perfect size and he loved the way she murmured—half hum of delight, half growling purr—when he squeezed her in just the right way. She'd arched back into him, rolling her hips in a circle against him and, bam, they were at it again.

He'd barely gotten the condom on—thank God she had a whole box—and then he'd entered her from behind while fingering her from the front.

She'd gasped at his penetration, but then quickly fell into his rhythm. And once again, he'd found something especially wonderful about her. As she built to climax, whether they were going slow or extra fast, her entire body entered the process.

And from this angle, he got to watch it all. He could see how her eyes fluttered with the building waves, how her hands clutched the sheets when she couldn't reach him. Even her toes got into the process as she wrapped her legs back around his, her toes curling tight into his body. Damn, she was flexible! And so incredibly beautiful.

He was able to delay his release as he focused on her. But the moment she began to contract, he lost all control and let himself go. Grabbing her undulating hips, he rammed into her one last time and exploded. Again. This was hands down the best night of his entire life.

Twenty minutes later, he felt her murmur something against his arm. She had to repeat twice before he understood her.

"We were supposed to meditate."

"I touched heaven. Does that count?"

She chuckled, her body shaking slightly—comfortably—against his. "I think you touched it a couple times."

"I still am," he said as he tightened his belly and thrust a bit, letting sensation roll through his consciousness. He was still buried deep inside her, but lassitude was making his brain fog out.

"God," she said as he felt her eyelashes flutter closed against his skin. "You are *so* not gay."

He tucked her tighter against him, then closed his own eyes. "We better do this again in the morning," he said. "Just in case I've been faking it the whole time."

He fell asleep to her laugh.

HE WOKE TO THE SOUND of a blender. A really loud, high-powered blender. It took him a moment to orient to the strange futon, strange room, strange…everything. Lord, his entire body hadn't felt as relaxed and happy since he was a kid on the first day of summer vacation. He stretched slowly, letting his body come awake with the movement while his mind scrambled to remember.

Oh, yeah. Elevator. Yoga. Bedroom snuggling. Best Night Ever. His smile grew as the blender finally switched off, and he scrambled out of bed. Two minutes later, he was pulling on his trousers and anticipating the Best Saturday Ever when a male voice penetrated the thin bedroom door. The words were spoken rapid-fire in a kind of manic desperation, and Roger leaned forward to hear better.

"Come on, Doc. You know these are the best there are. Handmade. Beautiful. You want the whole lot—I can see that you do. Isn't this beautiful? Quality. I'll sell you the whole lot for a couple thousand. Seriously. A steal."

Roger opened the bedroom door quietly. He only wore his trouser pants, not seeing the need to pull on his shirt. He located Amber immediately. She was in the kitchen pouring some green smoothielike substance into a glass while at the breakfast bar, a lanky twentysomething with sagging jeans shifted his weight back and forth between his two feet. Before him stretched a long line of dream catchers of all sizes, some quite elaborate.

"See how beautiful they are? This is fine quality work, you know. Look at these stones! Come on, Doc. Look at them!"

Amber obediently looked at the ornaments. She even stroked a finger across the feather of one of the larger ones. Then she passed the man a tall glass of puke-green smoothie.

"Aw, come on, Doc. You know this drink is crap."

Amber didn't answer. Just poured herself another glass and began to sip.

"What about the dream thingies, Doc?" the man continued. "Quality, huh? Real quality."

Again, Amber didn't speak, just stood there drinking her smoothie. Roger stepped into the room, moving toward the breakfast bar. She saw him immediately, her eyes lighting with warmth. Her visitor, however, still had his back to Roger as he continued to bounce back and forth on his feet.

"Tell you what, tell you what, Doc. I'll give it to you for eight hundred. It's a steal, I'm telling you. And it hurts me to do this. Seriously. But I like you. You been real nice to me, so I'm going to cut you a break."

Amber turned and pulled out another tall glass from her cabinet. Roger noted with pleasure that she wore yet another yoga outfit, and the fitted bottoms gave him all sorts of wonderful ideas. Much less wonderful was the way her visitor stilled for a moment, no doubt watching exactly the same sleek tush that Roger had noticed.

A surge of possessive instinct tightened Roger's muscles. He moved faster now, coming to Amber's side to wrap an arm around her hips and draw her close. It was a domination move accented by a kiss on her lips that was more for the newcomer than Amber. Not that she didn't seem to enjoy his kiss, but Roger's attention remained fixed on the other guy.

"Good morning," Roger said when they were done, his gaze warming as he looked into her eyes.

"Good morning to you," she returned. Then she pushed him away. "And stop being such a possessive Neanderthal. Roger, this is Spike. Spike, my friend Roger."

Okay, so she had known exactly what he was doing when he'd greeted her. He felt a twinge of guilt over that, but this Spike guy made him nervous. The man looked even worse up close. Unshaven, dirty, and with a hardness in his eyes that worried Roger. Still, he kept his tone neutral as he faced the man.

"Spike, huh? Did your mother really give you that name?"

"Nah. But everyone calls me Spike 'cause I look like that dude on *Buffy*. I'm mean and fast. People are afraid of me."

Like James Marsters? Only if the actor lost thirty pounds,

got bags under his eyes and slept in his own piss for a week. But Roger didn't say any of that. He just arched a brow and looked over the array of dream catchers on the counter. They were beautiful.

"So these are yours?" He allowed skepticism to color his tone.

"Yeah, yeah." Spike tried to slide into a coy look. "And the doc wants them real bad. If a guy wanted to get in her good graces, then he might buy them for her. So she can resell them to her patients, you know, and make a killing."

Roger allowed a cold smile to settle onto his features. "I don't think I need any help getting into her good graces."

Then Amber spoke, her voice low and soothing. "Who made them, Spike? Who made the dream catchers?" Roger found himself turning to her, a frown on his face. Her words seemed to have a weight to them, a power for no obvious reason. It wasn't in her tone or even her body stance, but when she spoke, both he and Spike turned to listen.

"A girl," Spike answered, his voice ratcheting up. "Got them from her cheap so I can turn that cheap on to you. Five hundred, Doc. And I'll even drink your green crap."

So saying, he reached over and started gulping her smoothie. Amber smiled and she motioned to the glass she had set in front of Roger.

"That one's yours."

Roger did his best not to look at the color, but it was in his mind as he took his first tentative sip. Nice. Fruity and a little sweet, but in a healthy, non-sugary, almost tasty kind of way. Spike finished his with a loud gasp, then he wiped his mouth with his sleeve.

"So, Doc. Ya got cash? I mean, I trust you and all. Your checks are good by me, but cash is always better. Saves me from going all the way to the bank, you know."

Amber didn't respond except to sort through the pile of

dream catchers until she finally lifted up one of the smaller ones. Flipping it over, she read a white tag that fluttered underneath. "Sweet Dreams handcrafted by Moira. She's even got a website listed."

Now Spike was visibly nervous and he leaned forward across the bar, his expression verging on aggressive. "I need the money, Doc. You gotta pay me for those before you start poking around in them."

She sighed. "I'm not buying stolen goods, Spike. But I will trade you for the whole lot. I'll do a couple of sessions on you to try and help you out. I won't even go to the police."

Spike's reaction was as fast as it was violent. He lunged across the breakfast bar screaming, "I didn't steal nothing!" Roger barely had time to get a hand up in front of Amber by way of protection. It wasn't all that helpful—Spike was stopped more by the breakfast bar than anything else. It gave Roger time to step fully between Amber and the psychopath.

"I think it's time you left, Spike," Roger said coldly.

Spike fell backward, shifting with scary speed into apologetic. "I'm sorry. I'm sorry. I just get angry when people mal-inform my good name, you know? You know?"

Spike tried to angle around Roger to look at Amber, but Roger kept himself firmly between the two. Meanwhile, Spike couldn't seem to stop talking.

"I didn't take the stuff, Doc. I'm not that kind of guy. I'm not! But I'm kinda in a bad fix, Doc. I need money or they're gonna hurt me. You hear that, Doc? They're gonna cut me if I don't pay. Just a few grand, Doc. I know you got the money."

That was it for Roger. The guy was a real and present danger. So he maneuvered around the breakfast bar and started bodily advancing on Spike. He didn't have any illusions if it came to a fight. Roger might be larger and more athletic, but Spike was fast and likely very wiry. Plus he was obviously desperate. A lucky blow and Roger would be on the ground. But that was a risk Roger was willing to take.

"You need to leave now," he said as forcefully as possible.

"And you need to get out of my face!" Spike said, pushing back with a punch hard enough to make Roger grunt but not give ground.

"Stop it! Both of you!" snapped Amber as she came around the breakfast bar.

"Stay back, Amber!" Roger ordered, not that she listened to him. Instead, she turned her attention to Spike.

"You don't have to live like this, Spike. You can change. You have to try!"

"They're gonna cut me!" Spike spat at her.

Amber took a deep breath, guilt and fear obvious in her features. "God, Spike, then get out of town! Start over!"

"There ain't nowhere to run! I need money!" he shot back, then he lunged for Amber. A full body leap that Roger was barely able to catch. But he did catch the man and using all of his strength, he spun the bastard around and started marching him out the door.

"I'll do a session," called Amber, her voice tinged with despair. "I know that sounds ridiculous, but it's all I can do."

"Get off of me, man!" growled Spike as he jerked and twisted in Roger's grip. But Roger didn't give way. He just kept marching the guy to the front door. "I gotta get the catchers, man! Just let me get the catchers!"

"The police will get them," Roger growled. "In fact the doc's calling 911 right now," he said, praying it was true.

"No, Doc, I wouldn't hurt you! I just need the catchers. Get off of me, you—" Spike launched into a string of profanities. Roger tightened his grip and shot Amber a grateful look as she pulled open her apartment door. Sadly, there was no cell phone in her hand. She obviously hadn't dialed 911.

Roger marshaled all of his strength and shoved Spike out the door. The man stumbled, but recovered fast enough, whipping around with a snarl. At that moment, Roger had to admit to a real resemblance between Spike and his vampire namesake. Fortunately, he didn't have to fight the bastard. Just as Spike was gathering himself to run back inside, Roger managed to grab the door and slam it shut. Spike didn't make it through, hitting the metal with a loud thud. He did, however, stay there, banging on the door and hurling profanities through it.

Meanwhile, Roger turned back to Amber, his gaze scanning her from head to toe. "Are you all right?"

She looked pale, shaken, and her arms were wrapped protectively around her torso, but she managed to nod. "I'm fine. Thanks. Are you okay? Did he kick you or anything?"

Yes. The bastard had managed to land a few well-placed whacks, but nothing that wouldn't heal. "I'm fine. So where's my phone? I'll call 911 now, though you should have done it five minutes ago. What were you thinking letting him in here?"

She sighed, wincing as Spike jerked on the door. The thing held, but who knew for how long. So Roger turned toward the door and bellowed, "The police are on their way! I suggest you get lost now!"

Another loud round of curses was screeched through the door, but then there were heavy footfalls running away. Spike had apparently given up, and Roger released a breath in relief.

"His mother lives down the block," Amber said, her voice apologetic. "She asked me to do some energy work on her son. To help him past his gambling addiction."

"Yeah," Roger drawled as he crossed to the kitchen. "That obviously worked out great."

"You think I don't know that?" snapped Amber and Roger

immediately felt contrite. After all, it wasn't her fault that she lived in a neighborhood of addicts and nut jobs. But she really needed to move. Like yesterday.

"Sorry," he said. "I know you're doing your best."

She shot him an irritated look, but didn't comment. Instead, she stomped over to her kitchen and lifted up her own glass of yuck-green smoothie. He felt even worse when he saw that her hand was shaking as she took a sip.

Crossing to her side, he enveloped her in a hug. She resisted at first, but in the end, she relaxed into his arms. She even returned the hug with one hand.

"I'm sorry," he said into her hair. "It's not your fault. I've just never woken up to a psychopath before."

She pushed out of his arms, and he reluctantly let her go. "Spike's not a psychopath. He's just addicted to gambling. And that's taking the predictable course." She grabbed Spike's empty glass and took it to the sink to wash it. "God, what am I going to say to his mother? She thinks I can wave my fingers and have her son magically heal. I'm doing my best, but he's got to take some responsibility for the addiction."

Roger stared at her, wondering at her odd reaction to the situation. First of all, she was calm. A lot calmer than he felt right then. Which meant she probably faced situations like this all the time. And if that wasn't scary as hell, he didn't know what was.

Then there was her bizarre statement about sessions and Spike's mother. Did she really think that living foods and energy mumbo jumbo could heal a *gambling addiction?*

Honesty forced him to admit that she obviously did *not* think that. After all, she'd just said Spike had to take some responsibility himself. Well, duh. But the dullness in her body language told him something was weighing her down. She obviously thought she'd failed the boy. But rather than argue, he gestured to her locked metal cabinet.

"Can you give me back my phone? We need to call the police."

She carefully did not look up from the dishes. "We don't need to call the police."

"We sure as hell do," he answered firmly. How had he known she was going to argue with him?

She shook her head. "I'll get in touch with Moira whomever she is through her website. We can get her back her dream catchers that way. Spike's going to have enough problems without us adding the police on top of everything."

"He *stole* those dream catchers. He *threatened* you. And now he's so desperate that he'll probably hold up a liquor store or something. At this point, the police are his only hope of surviving until tomorrow and not killing someone else in the process."

She didn't answer, but he saw the stubbornness in every line of her body.

"Amber!"

She turned back to face him, slumping against the sink as she did. "I just keep thinking about his mother."

"Well, don't," he returned. "Come on, Amber. Spike has created this problem. Enabling his addiction is the opposite of helping him and you know it."

"I'm not enabling! I'm just—"

"Shielding him from the police and keeping him from facing the consequences of his violence? Amber, think! He's going to hurt someone else!"

He saw the knowledge in her face. In truth, it had been there all the time, but she'd needed him to force her to face it. Not a problem for him, so long as she eventually got to a rational place. She got there in less than a minute, and soon she was fishing a key out of her pocket. A moment later, he was talking to the police while Amber curled up on her couch and Roger watched her with a worried frown.

The woman who had approached him in the elevator yesterday had been all business and cool confidence. Last night's dinner had shown him a warmer woman with a nurturing streak a mile wide. But neither event had prepared him for the woman he saw now. She was unnaturally still on the couch, her expression carefully blanked. She appeared to be waiting—for him to get off the phone, for the police to arrive and take their statement, for God only knew what else. And she appeared not so much lost as defeated. Slowly, but inevitably, defeated. Like a stone worn down by steady, grinding pressure.

And that sight bothered him more than anything Spike had said or done.

10

ROGER'S CAR WAS TRASHED. Amber had walked outside to get a breath of fresh air, away from the cops, away from her growing doubts, away from everything for just a moment. Roger had shot her an anxious look as she stepped out, but he was occupied with the police, giving his statement. So she'd slipped outside into the afternoon glare only to see what had been done to Roger's car.

The windows were all smashed in. A door was dented as if someone had kicked it repeatedly. And when that hadn't worked, someone had scratched key marks all the way around it. That someone was obviously Spike, and the whole thing just made Amber sad. Bone-deep sad.

"Well, hell," groaned a voice behind her just before large hands framed her waist. It was Roger as he realized the extent of the damage to his car.

"At least you didn't get a ticket for parking in front of a hydrant," she said.

"Well, then everything's okay," he said as he stepped around in front of her, his eyes worried. "Are you okay?"

She blinked. "Your car just got thoroughly trashed and you're asking about me?"

"I have insurance for my car. So, yeah, I'm asking about you."

She smiled, touched. "I'm fine."

"Really? Because I gotta say, you don't seem so fine."

She took a deep breath, consciously centering herself back in the *now*. She was healthy on a beautiful day. She'd had a fabulous night last night. And best of all, the reason for the fabulous night was standing in front of her, looking at her as if she were—well, if not the most important thing in his life, at least in the top three. Life was good. She was good. She just had to hold on to that.

She forced her lips into a curve and said with as much confidence as she could muster, "I'm really fine, Roger. And you probably want to get home and change. And, um, call your insurance agent."

He gave a rueful grimace, then gestured to one of the cops leaving her building. "I believe I have another crime to report," he said to the officer. Then he turned back and looked at her. "Go and get a bag packed. Whatever you need. I'll finish up with the police and call a tow truck. Then we'll go get something sinfully delicious for lunch before settling in at my place."

She smiled, her heart and her soul warmed. God, he really was the nicest man. And if it were a couple years ago, she would have already had her bags packed. She didn't want to admit it, but Spike had rattled her in more ways than one. But she was stronger than her fears. She would not turn tail and run away. She was going to stand her ground and stay in her home.

Fortunately, she didn't have to say any of that. The police officer came forward, grimly flipping a page over in his notebook. Amber took that moment to duck back inside. She wasn't going to pack, but she wasn't going to fight about it either. Certainly not out there on the street anyway. So she stepped back up into her apartment and ran right smack dab into Mary.

"Oh, my God, Amber, oh, my God! What happened? Why are the police here? Oh, my—"

"Hello, Mary. How are you feeling today?" The doctor in Amber eyed her friend critically, picking out the symptoms of rheumatoid arthritis. Mary seemed to be walking better and her hands didn't seem so cramped. That was good news.

"Oh, well, I'm out of bed, see. And I thought I should take a walk and thank you for taking over my plant duties yesterday. You said I should get out more. Enjoy the sun when I can, and you were so right. But then I saw the police cars and I had to rush over. Well, rush as fast as I can go, you know. Everyone's talking about it. Did Spike really attack you? And who is that man in the suit with the poor car? Was he staying over? Amber..."

Her words went on and on, like a babbling brook of sounds. But they held more life and energy than Amber had heard in a long time from her friend, so she smiled as they walked together back into Amber's home.

The words continued, and soon another person was adding more. Sandy from down the hall came with her daughter, just to check on Doc Crystal. With the police outside, everyone inside the building felt safe in slipping in to find out what had happened.

Amber told them the short version, explaining that Spike's gambling had gotten him into a bad situation. He had not hurt her, but he was desperate. If anyone saw him, they should stay away and call the police immediately. That was all she said, but it sparked long discussions about addictions and desperate people. Then they shifted to things that could go wrong in a person's life, and from there to other neighborhood gossip while she made some more green smoothies and passed them around. For some, this would be the healthiest food they'd have all day, and she didn't mind the task. The noise of the blender, thankfully, kept her from adding to the conversation. And so it went until Roger came back upstairs.

Everyone went silent the moment he walked in, their speculative gazes hopping from him to Amber and back. And for his part, his eyes widened in surprise at the collection of people he saw on her couch, on her floor and leaning against her breakfast bar. But he was nothing if not suave. He smiled warmly to everyone and carefully shut the door behind him before addressing the group.

"Well, I'm certainly relieved to see that you have a lot of friends here to watch out for you," he said by way of greeting.

"Oh, we're all here for Doc Crystal!" piped in Josie, Sandy's daughter.

He didn't say anything, but Amber saw his eyes flicker with emotion. She could almost hear his thoughts all the way across the room. He knew as well as she did that her friends would disappear the moment anything resembling danger or the police returned to her doorstep. It wasn't that they were bad people. They just had a lot of things on their mind, enough troubles on their plate. Too many to be willing to leap into her issues.

Fortunately, he didn't say any of that, and Amber wisely cut off any opportunity by coming out from behind the breakfast bar. "Everyone, this is my friend Roger. He's—"

"Oh! You're from that robotics company!" piped in Mary.

"Yes—" began Roger, but Mary wasn't going to be stopped.

"Well, my God, Amber, you get all the luck. I've been watering the plants there for months and never came home with anything as fine as—"

"Mary!" exclaimed at least three people, including Amber.

"What?" protested Mary. "I'm just saying…"

Roger took up the thread. "That I should have looked at my company's plant care personnel much sooner. I can't disagree with that!"

Not surprisingly, Mary blushed a pretty pink. Meanwhile, Roger touched Amber's waist in a purposely intimate gesture.

"Well, as much as I hate to break this up, Amber and I need to get going. Thank you all for stopping by. I'm glad the doc has people she can count on in an emergency."

Amber glanced at him, trying to gauge his words. Was he being sarcastic? She couldn't tell. Either way, she didn't argue. As uncomfortable as she made her home—with a decor defined by its lack of furniture—she still tended to gather neighbors. If she had enough chairs for them all, they'd never leave. So she didn't say a word as Roger managed to tease, cajole and charm everyone out the door. He was smooth, she'd give him that. And sweet. And overprotective. And so she'd tell him the moment he tried to order her out of her home.

That moment came about three seconds after he shut the door behind her friends. "Wow, they sure like to talk," he gasped. Then he peered into her bedroom. "So where's your bag? The tow truck's been and gone. I just need to grab my briefcase and your bag, then we can go. I gotta say, I'm starved! What do you think of Italian…?" His voice trailed away when he realized she hadn't moved from where she was leaning against the breakfast bar.

"Oh, hell," he said. "You're about to be stubborn, aren't you?"

She smiled, letting her weariness show in her face. "Thank you for everything you've done, Roger. I couldn't have managed Spike alone or the police. You were wonderful."

He smiled. "So thank me over a big pile of lasagna."

She shook her head.

"No lasagna? Fine. We'll eat more salad. But I'm telling you, it's going to have to be a *lot* of salad. I'm starved."

"Actually," she said as she moved to her refrigerator, "I made some lasagna just the other day." It was raw-food lasagna, made out of zucchini slices and pureed tomatoes. Which meant it looked like the favorite Italian dish, but tasted nothing like it.

"Amber," he said, his voice dropping low. "Come on, you can't stay here. Spike could come back at any moment."

"Then it's a good thing I keep my door locked and have a cell phone to call the police."

"Amber—"

"This is my home, Roger. It's my sanctuary."

"And it's a great home, but for the moment, wouldn't you rather feel safe? Just until Spike is caught?"

She didn't have an answer to that. The chatter from her friends had kept her from thinking about being there alone after Roger had left. But she'd have to face her fear sometime. "I can't hide every time something scares me."

"I'm not talking about every time. I'm talking about this time. For now. Until Spike is picked up again by the police."

Amber shook her head. "He's not going to come back. There isn't anything here for him."

"There's money here—"

"Ha!" she snorted.

"*He* thinks there is," Roger pressed. "Don't you remember? He said he knew you had the cash."

"He's delusional."

"Probably," Roger agreed. "But that doesn't mean he won't come looking. Maybe this time with a gun."

Amber crossed her arms over her chest, fighting the fear that had started creeping up her spine. "You're just trying to scare me into going home with you."

Roger shook his head. "The cops said the same thing. And I'm adding that it's better to be safe than sorry." He stepped forward and brushed his hands along the outside of her arms. "Come on. This just makes sense. I swear I won't jump you. Unless you want me to, of course."

Oh, she'd want him to. Not right now, but all too soon, she was sure of it. But that wasn't the problem. There was something else holding her back. And because he wasn't a fool, he noticed that right away.

"What is it that you're worried about? Honestly."

She bit her lip and tried to think. And when her mind twisted in on itself without shedding any light, she simply closed her eyes and took a deep breath. She purposely quieted her thoughts and allowed the truth to form out of the silence.

"I've been thinking hard about my life lately. Wondering if I made the wrong choice so long ago in coming to Chicago."

He nodded. "Big life questions. I understand. A scare like today can bring that on."

She smiled. "Yeah, but it's not just that. I mean, it is that, but in a larger sense. I'm a healer at heart. That's who I've always been. I want to heal people." She gestured to her home and the neighborhood at large. "I came here because traditional medicine wasn't answering my questions. Because the politics was interfering with the healing. And because I wanted to explore the places Western medicine wasn't looking."

"And now you're wondering if everything you've done has been a whole big waste of time."

She arched a brow. "Yeah."

He gestured to the doorway. "It didn't look like those people thought you'd wasted your time. They looked like you were part of their lives in a good way."

She smiled, reassured but not enough. "Thank you for that, but—"

"But you don't know if that's enough. You don't know if all your research and explorations have done anything but tanked your medical career."

Her eyes widened; she was surprised that he could so clearly read her thoughts.

He laughed, his expression wry. "It's not like that's a hard thing to figure out. I mean, you obviously feel like you failed with Spike. You've given up a lot to pursue your passion. It's not surprising that after this morning, you'd be wondering if it's worth it."

Overwhelmed by his understanding, she gave him an impulsive hug. He responded in kind, wrapping her in his arms until she felt like she never wanted to leave. Then his voice came rumbling through to her, his words gentle, coaxing.

"What I don't understand," he said, "is why all those thoughts are keeping you from going to my house where you can cogitate, ponder and meditate on these thoughts in safety."

She smiled, amused by his phrasing. Personally, she'd have to add "angst" and "worry" to the list of what she was likely to do as she sorted through her feelings. But that's not what forced her to push away from him. It was the knowledge that she ought to face these thoughts without his distracting presence. She couldn't make life decisions while a man as gorgeous as him was a breath away.

But she wasn't ready to tell him that, so she reached for something else. Something logical, but not the real reason. "You live in a high-rise condo, right?"

He nodded.

"You probably have the works. Huge TV, stereo sound, espresso machine?"

"I gave away the machine when I gave up caffeine."

She snorted. Like that made any difference at all. He still lived the life she'd left behind. The life that could look way too appealing after months of living in a converted warehouse. "Your life, your space, is everything I used to be. High energy, high pressure, high stress."

He arched a brow. "So?"

"So going back to that is making the decision. It's choosing all the trappings of that life over what I've created here. I'm not ready to do that. I'm not ready to say everything I've done here is worthless."

"And you think spending a night with my leather couch is going to do all that?"

Put like that, she sounded ridiculous. "Look, I started this little dance," she said, feeling her way through her words. "I wanted to remember it all again. I had fun putting on the designer boots and makeup. I loved the negotiation with Jack, and the hot sex in the elevator was beyond fantastic. But it was a trip down memory lane for me. And now it's done."

He touched her face, caressing her cheek before finally cupping her chin. She should have known he was about to switch tactics. Worse, she should have known from the beginning the way he would find to make her cave.

"You know, this is really bad for my blood pressure. If I leave now, I'm going to spend the rest of the night worrying about you."

"Don't be silly—"

"I'm not being silly! Amber, I can already feel my blood vessels throbbing. That's a sure sign that my blood pressure is up dangerously high."

Yes, it was, and she was immediately worried about him. "Look, you need to sit down."

He stubbornly shook his head. "What I need to do is get you somewhere safe until Spike is caught."

"Roger—"

"Amber, please. Just for tonight. So I won't stroke out on your floor."

She sighed. He had her there. She'd seen his regular readings and knew that a stroke wasn't out of the question. This close, she could see the steady beat in his temple.

"You don't play fair," she groused.

"Not when it's important," he said with a cocky grin. But then he sobered. "I'd be happy to talk to you about your life choices, about all of it—the research, the living space, even the psychopath addicts. We can examine it all in minute detail. Let's just do it somewhere safe."

But would she do the thinking she needed to? Or would they end up in couples yoga again? "I really need to think, Roger."

"Great. Do it at my place because I'm going to pester you until you do."

That was obviously true. So she caved. She'd go just for one night. She'd see if they actually got some serious thinking done or more hot monkey sex. And truthfully, she thought with a wry grin, would the second choice be all that bad?

"Fine," she said. "But we're taking the fake lasagna. And you're going to meditate tonight."

He grinned. "Not a problem."

"That's meditation without the sex," she snapped.

He huffed. "Spoilsport."

She gave him a stern look that he appeared to take at face value. Silly him. She knew better than anyone just how impossible it was to resist him. But for both their sakes, she had to remain firm. They both needed to examine their lives. He needed to find out what was making his blood pressure soar and she needed to find a better way to do her life's work. Because living on the edge of poverty just wasn't working.

"No sex," she repeated in an undertone as she went into the bedroom to pack a bag. "Not even if I beg."

11

AMBER STEPPED INTO Roger's apartment and half snorted, half laughed. He turned, his brows arched in question and she tried to wave it away. But he didn't let her off the hook, so she finally confessed the truth.

"I can absolutely feel that this is your apartment," she said.

"What, because the decor suits me?" He gestured to the clean modern lines. Electronics abounded, fabrics were soft browns with a few red accents and, of course, everything was dominated by a huge desk set up in the spare bedroom. Piles of papers were spilling out of that room into the main living area. She counted four stacks of books, a haphazard stack of brochures and the like, plus a tennis racquet perched on top of an old monitor that was probably on its way to the home for unwanted electronics.

"Well, yes, it does. But that's not what I meant." She stepped deeper into the living room and tried to take a deep breath. She couldn't. The energy of this space was frenetic, cluttered and filled with all his thinking, thinking, thinking. "There's a lot of mind here."

He blinked. "You sound like that's a bad thing."

She shrugged, knowing he wasn't going to flow with what

she said, but feeling compelled to explain anyway. "Thinking is great. But it's easy for it to spiral out of control. And your mind, my friend, spins and spins and spins."

He snorted at her answer, but then sobered when he realized she wasn't teasing him. She remained silent, giving him time to work out whatever he needed to. He set down her duffle bag.

"I thought you wanted me to think. About my life and… whatever."

She nodded. "But I wonder if there's room in your brain for more thinking. You understand that's what meditation is for, right? To empty out the thinking to allow space for better."

He arched her brow. "Better?"

"For God."

His face carefully blanked, and she knew he was terrified she was going to morph into an evangelist, so she rushed to reassure him.

"I'm not talking organized religion, unless that's what works for you. I'm saying there is something that is more than what our thinking can dream up. There is something beyond your mind. And unless your mind shuts up, you will never hear what else is out there."

He shook his head as he moved into his apartment. "You are the strangest person I've ever met."

"Because I talk about God and mind and space?"

"Because you make sense in the oddest ways." He folded his arms and frowned at her. Not in anger. It was more like confusion. "You're a doctor, and yet you're not. You're nurturing in a way that will probably get you killed, and yet the woman that wowed me in the elevator was the furthest thing from a mother figure I've ever seen." He took a step forward, his body crowding into hers. But she didn't shy backward. The air was too electric—too delicious—for her to run. "I can't figure you out," he finally said.

"That's because there isn't space in your mind for me."

"That's total bull," he said with a laugh. "I've got plenty of thoughts about you."

She put her hand on his chest, pushing him gently backward. She wasn't ready for another bout of high-energy sex with him. Well, her body was ready. Her body was *always* ready around him. But her mind was beginning to spin just like his, and that would end up with her like a whirling dervish. And once she got to that place, who knew what havoc she would cause?

"Let's eat, Roger. And then we'll see about the rest."

He arched his brows, his mind going straight to the obvious. "Really?"

She laughed. "Food. Now."

ROGER CHEWED HIS "living food lasagna" with what he thought was good grace. Amber's peal of laughter told him differently.

"You know," he grumbled, "this doesn't taste anything like real lasagna."

It had long strips of cucumber in place of noodles, crushed cashews for the cheese, smooshed tomatoes for the sauce and then a whole lot of other weirdness going on. All in all, it looked like lasagna only because it was layered and had some red stuff in it. And it wasn't even served hot, which made it a weird-looking salad in his book, not a favorite Italian meal.

She smiled. "Yeah, I know. The recipe calls it lasagna because of what it looks like. And because calling it zucchini strips with cashews and tomatoes doesn't sound as interesting."

He frowned down at his plate. "This is zucchini?"

"Yup."

"Huh. I hate zucchini. Have since I was a kid."

"Do you hate the meal?"

He looked at her, letting his expression say it all.

"Bet you'd hate stroking out even more."

He stabbed his fork into the damned vegetables. "There's dying and then there's living your life such that you wish you were dead."

She laughed, and he realized that he'd eat a ton of weird lasagna-shaped salad just to hear that sound again. Gone was the lost woman who'd sat on her couch waiting for the police. In her place sat a woman who smiled at him, her expression warm with sympathy even as her eyes danced with humor.

"Look, I know this is hard," she said, "but there is something better on the horizon."

He glanced up. "Let me guess. Spaghetti made out of cucumbers? Hamburger from crushed bean pâté? Or better yet, cheesecake made from two kumquats and a pistachio?"

Her laughter rang deeper and longer, and he found himself smiling at the sound.

"My, that sounds interesting. You should become a chef."

"A chef. Of food that isn't cooked."

She nodded. "I have ten cookbooks on food that isn't actually cooked."

He frowned. "I can't tell if you're teasing me or not."

"Not. I'll show them to you when I get back to my loft."

He shook his head. "That's just wrong. Flat out wrong."

She leaned back in her seat, apparently full. He did, too, not because he was full but because he couldn't stomach more of it. She patted his hand.

"Give it three weeks. Your new taste buds will have kicked in by then."

He blinked. "Taste buds? I get new taste buds?"

"Yup. For life. As in, you can taste the life in foods."

He simply stared at her, his mind boggling at the thought.

"I'm not joking," she said. "I can actually taste life in my food. It's not that I don't like fish or bread or a good steak, though it's been years since I had red meat. But whenever I taste them now, they seem dead to me. Like eating Styrofoam. Even weird lasagna tastes great to me because it's bursting with life. I don't have any other word for it. It's alive, and it satisfies me as nothing else does."

He looked at her, seeing that she was serious but unable to imagine what she meant. How did one taste life?

"Give it three weeks, Roger. You'll see what I mean."

He rolled his eyes. "Okay, let's examine my options here. Medically speaking, exactly how bad would a stroke be? Sure, part of my brain would die, I might start drooling onto my lap and be unable to carry on a real conversation. But on the other hand, at that point, I wouldn't really care what I was eating, right? You could feed me all the leaves you want."

She stood up and dropped a kiss on his forehead. "If you're finished, we should really start looking at your meditation practice."

He straightened, happily abandoning his lunch. "If it's anything like our yoga practice, then I'm game!"

She shot him a look, and he held up his hands, already knowing what she was thinking. How freaky was that? They were already close enough that he could read her thoughts?

"I was joking!" he said. "I am taking this seriously."

She arched her brows at him and he tried to look sincere.

"I really am! Trust me, there's no way you could get me to eat that lunch unless I was taking this seriously. But between you and me, I think it's more likely that my skin will turn green before I taste life."

She laughed. "Well, if you do, I promise to write you up in a medical journal. You'll be famous as the first green-skinned human."

"But I'll be green."

She shrugged. "Fame has its costs."

So did high blood pressure, but he wasn't going to bring that up again. Instead, he ordered himself as sternly as possible to man up. After all, he was doing this for a reason, and it wasn't just to have hot sex with his new yoga instructor. He had to do something drastic. That meant salad and meditation. Even if it killed him.

Amber had already pulled two large cushions onto the floor. She sat on one and leaned her back against the front of the couch. Then she extended her legs out in front of her and let her hands drop loosely onto her thighs. He eyed her with a frown.

"You're not going to ask me to get into the lotus position, are you? I don't think my knees work that way."

"Neither do mine," she said. "I don't even like going cross-legged because my feet go numb."

"So what do I do?"

She indicated the cushion beside her. "Just sit down. Get comfortable. But not so comfortable you could fall asleep."

He nodded and got into place. Like her, his back was braced on the couch, his legs were extended before him. As meditation positions went, this was rather comfortable. In fact, he'd once spent some hours just like this, only he'd been playing a new video game at the time.

"Now what?" he asked.

And so began her lesson. It was really rather simple. She gave him a ton of different possible mantras or other tricks, but it all added up to emptying his mind and just breathing. Eventually, so the theory went, his mind would learn to be quiet and that would create space for something cool. Something divine. Or just something that would lower his blood pressure. That was the plan and he fully embraced it.

Up until the moment he fell asleep.

AMBER OPENED HER EYES when she heard Roger's low, steady snore. She couldn't help but smile. First, he looked adorable, all rumpled and exhausted. Second, she remembered her first serious attempts at meditation. She had been so chronically exhausted, she'd fallen asleep at least half the time.

But most of all she smiled because it was Roger sitting beside her, trying to do what she asked. Sure, he had a huge incentive, but it didn't seem to matter to her heart. He listened to her, even when he didn't really believe a word she was saying. He was eating weird food that she'd taken months to warm up to. And he was the most gifted lover she'd ever had. All in all, that made him one hot package.

She pushed up to her feet. As long as he was sleeping, she could do some deeper sessions while he wasn't distracting her. And then, of course, she would have to do a little self-examination of her own. Because while Roger had been showering and she was supposedly setting up lunch, she'd used his computer to check her email.

Right at the top was a note from Jack at Mandolin. Her old boss—Bob the Boob—was retiring. Jack thought now was the perfect time to come back. She could get hired on while the committee was still searching for a replacement. After all, the Smithson name still held a lot of power at Mandolin.

And just like that, her old life was within her grasp. With just a little bit of work, she might very well step back into the life she'd left behind minus Bob the Boneheaded Boss. It was exactly what she'd been maneuvering for, especially with the trip out to Mandolin already planned for two weeks from now.

Everything was exactly how she had angled to get it. But now that it was here, she was assailed by doubts. She glanced behind her at Roger sleeping so adorably. Did she really want to leave everything in Chicago behind?

12

ROGER WOKE UP to a sneezing fit that nearly blew his head off. Then he started coughing and snuffling to the point where he was sure he was getting a cold. Until it seemed to fade away. When he was done, he looked up to see Amber smiling beatifically at him from the coffee table. She was seated on the floor, pen and paper in front of her and a massive notebook open on the floor beside her.

"Wow, sneezes of the damned. What was that?" he asked, not really intending for her to answer. It was just all he could think of to say.

"You were getting rid of some bad energies," she said.

He nodded slowly, doing his best not to leap to his knee-jerk reaction. After all, how was he to know if he hadn't been doing exactly that: sneezing out some bad juju. Except, of course, his sneezes probably had more to do with the spring pollen than anything else. But he didn't say that. Instead, he rubbed his face and tried to clear his head. Then he jerked his chin at her writing.

"Whatcha doing?"

She set down her pen, then stretched, rolling her head

around, pulling her arms high, and generally making his brain fall straight south. God, she had the most amazing body.

"I just finished my session on Spike. It's not going to get him out of the hole he's dug, but maybe it'll help him find the strength to climb out."

He pulled his thoughts out of the gutter long enough to look at her paper. It was filled with notes and abbreviations that he couldn't understand. "You can work on him...on paper?"

She smiled. "Energy flows regardless of material boundaries. Otherwise, how would we get radio waves and the like?"

He shrugged. To his mind, radio waves and energy healing were two different animals. But he knew next to nothing about it. "So what's your success rate?"

She sighed. "Depends on your definition of success. Most of my clients see improvement, but not cures. Though there have been a few notable exceptions," she said, her eyes sparkling.

"Really?"

She nodded. "I've seen allergies disappear overnight, swollen joints regain full use, asthma shift from debilitating to almost gone. I'm really thrilled with this work." She pushed away a huge manual before shifting her legs into a stretch. And again, he had trouble concentrating on her words. "Out of everything I've studied, this is the one I like the most."

"So you have patients?"

She nodded. "But not nearly as many as I need to pay off the last of my medical school debt. But I'm hopeful of a solution soon."

He looked at her more closely, seeing the way her eyes slid away when she spoke. Obviously, she wasn't entirely comfortable with talking about whatever solution she saw in the works. He wanted to ask more, to find out exactly what she was thinking and doing. But right then, his stomach growled, long and loud.

"So I guess I'm hungry," he said with a laugh. "Or more like starved. You want anything?"

She shook her head. "I'm fine, but you're not used to this diet. Eat a banana. Or I could make you—"

"Not another salad. I'll go with a banana." And an apple. And any other thing in his kitchen that would qualify on this bizarro regimen. A quick rummage through his kitchen revealed that he didn't have nearly enough. "I need to go to the grocery store."

She had returned to her manual. "I've got a lot more to do here. Do you mind going to the store without me? I've made up a list."

She waved a page of notebook paper at him. He bit into the apple as he crossed to get the page. Looking down, he saw that it was a short list.

Any green leaves that you will eat
Kale
Any fruit that you will eat
Any raw nuts that you will eat

"Try for organic, if you can," she said as he frowned down at the list. "There's an organic market nearby. Just go there and go wild."

He waved the paper at her. "This does not sound like going wild to me. Going wild is—"

"Maybe we can try another yoga session after you shop," she said, waggling her eyebrows.

He paused, having to seriously weigh his options. Organic green things and more sex versus a normal diet but no nookie. He chose the sex, but it was a near thing.

"I'll be back in an hour," he said as he grabbed his keys.

"I'll be here. And I might even be naked."

His step hitched halfway out the door, and he fumbled to get out a pen.

"Roger?" she asked from her place on his floor.

"I'm just adding something to this list."

"Really? What?"

"Condoms."

"Oh! Right. Good idea."

He grinned at the blush that turned her cheeks so rosy. Okay, so endless salad was definitely worth it. He rushed out the door, resolved to make it back in a half hour, tops.

FOUR DAYS LATER, he was still grinning, even if they were back in her loft and not his apartment. Sure, he would kill for something meaty to sink his teeth into. Yes, he had spent way more time than he'd like listening to her neighbor complain about sciatica pains. And yes, Spike was still disturbingly missing. But all in all, the daily sexual adventures were more than making up for the other inconveniences.

And, miracle of miracles, his blood pressure was dropping. He was sure Amber thought it had to do with her energy sessions. Apparently, she worked on him daily, writing stuff down on paper and staring into space. Privately, he thought it had more to do with a freaking wonderful amount of sex. Either way, he wasn't complaining. Unless, of course, it was meal time. Damn, he was sick of smoothies and lukewarm food.

Then came the inexplicable moment of raw fury. A full-blown rage that rolled through him for no rational reason at all. The cause? The color of his tomato, of all things. He lost it. He completely lost his mind. His tomato was supposed to be orangy-red, but this particular cherry tomato was orangy-white and bruised. And it was one of a lot of cherry tomatoes that were subpar, in his opinion, for which he had paid an exorbitant amount. "Organic, my ass," he growled. "That just means they can charge five times as much for the crap normal grocery stores won't accept!"

Amber looked up from her salad. Being at her home tonight suddenly annoyed him even more. After all, his home had all his toys. Her home had a futon, for God's sake, and freaky neighbors.

Holy crap, he was nuts. He even knew he was being nuts as he started stomping about her loft while ranting about the poor quality of produce in the local health-food store. It was like he was standing outside of himself shaking his head at the freaky insano that was now inhabiting his body.

And Amber just sat there, her fork poised halfway to her mouth as she watched him. On her fork, of course, was one of the few perfect cherry tomatoes. Of course, she got the good ones. It was bad enough that he had to be on this stupid diet, but did she have to get all the *good* tomatoes?

"Oh. My. God!" he bellowed. "What the fuck is wrong with me?"

She set down her fork. "I was waiting for this to happen."

"Waiting? Waiting! You've been waiting for me to lose it completely? You should have let me know. I would have gone insane a couple days ago!"

Her lips quirked, but she didn't laugh. Good thing because he didn't know what he would do if she started guffawing at him. He ran his hands through his hair, trying not to grab hold and haul it out. He had to do something—anything—or he was going to explode. Meanwhile, Amber kept talking in her damned, calm, Doctor voice. It was enough to make him want to strangle her.

"Our tissues hold old energies—thoughts, feelings and whatnot. You've been detoxing for a little bit now. Apparently, you've just hit a pocket of anger."

"Anger?" he gasped. "Anger! It's more like a freaking murderous rage!'"

She arched her brows. "Really? Well, do tell. What are you feeling?"

Had she not heard him? *"Rage!"*

She nodded, her body and her expression sliding to that bland place she went to when one of her neighbors came in ranting about one thing or another. He'd seen it enough times now to recognize her actions. She went quiet and just let the rant run its course. It always did, and before long, the neighbor would thank her and leave.

He'd marveled at it before. He'd been impressed with the way she simply waited whomever out. He'd just never thought she'd have to do it with him. And the fact that she was staring calmly at him ratcheted up his fury yet another degree.

"Amber, do not do that silent thing with me!" he bellowed.

She arched her brow. "What silent thing?"

He didn't have the words to explain, so he just went back to pacing a circle around the couch. "Talk to me!"

"I'd much rather you talk to me, Roger. Tell me why you're feeling such rage."

"I don't know!" He threw up his hands. "The lettuce was poisoned. I'm having an aneurysm. Too much sex really does turn the brain to mush. *I don't know!*"

Her lips twitched and he rounded on her.

"Do not laugh at me! It's rude to laugh at the insane."

"You're not insane, Roger. Just try to empty your mind."

"I'm too pissed off."

"Fine. Then just feel the rage—"

"I am!"

"And let it wash through you. What is beneath the rage?"

"More rage."

"Fair enough. What's beneath that?"

He glared at her, fighting for the smallest iota of rationality. "I don't know what that means," he snapped.

"Get quiet, Roger. Just try. What's the first thing that comes to mind?"

That this was nuts and he needed to go boxing. He paused. Had he just thought of boxing? Jesus. He hadn't gone boxing since he was a kid. What the hell? But he looked down at his hands and they were clenched into fists. Yeah. He really wanted to punch something right then.

"Roger?"

He blinked and focused on her, scrambling to put words to the feelings crashing through him. "I want to hit things. Like in a boxing ring." And outside of a boxing ring. And just because he felt like hitting things.

"Do you box?"

"Never. Well, except for a few times when I was twelve. My friend's dad took us. I never understood the need before now. Jumping into a ring to beat the crap out of each other. I mean, it was fun as long as it was on a video game. But up close and personal, it was just stinky. And painful."

"Did you get beaten up?"

He shook his head. "No. We were just kids. But there was this one guy—all wiry and bouncy. Thinking back, he was probably jonesing or something. He had that nervous, unable to sit still, never shuts up kind of energy. To him, we were just fresh meat, someone to beat up."

"In the ring?"

Roger shook his head. "No. Like I said, we were just kids and my friend's dad was there trying to teach us stuff. But this other kid, he was like twenty, and he could have had us eating out of his hand. You know how it is with preteens. If there's an older guy who's halfway cool, you just hang out with him, hoping their cool rubs off."

"So you hung out with him?"

Roger rubbed a hand over his face, the memory hazy but the feelings so strong. "He was an ass. I can't even remember what he did. Probably called us names or something. Laughed at how we punched the bag."

"And that made you angry?"

Roger realized he was grinding his fist into his palm and he stared at his hands like they were alien things. He wasn't a guy who punched things.

"No. Well, I suppose. He was just a jerk. And he made us both feel stupid, I guess." He looked at her, his eyes narrowed in disbelief. "You can't possibly think my blood pressure is tied to some jerk who hassled us when I was twelve."

She shrugged. "It's your memory. Tell me what it means to you."

He threw up his hands. "It means that twelve is a sucky age. Old enough to know that the world's screwed up, but too puny and too dumb to do anything about it. Thank God, I'm not there anymore."

She arched her brow at him. "I kinda enjoyed twelve. Got to put on my older sister's makeup, but nobody laughed if I disappeared with my Barbies. At twelve, you can still be a little kid if you want, but you can play grown-up without the responsibilities."

He arched a brow at her. "Well, maybe it's that way for girls, but us guys are too busy trying to prove we're macho by that point. Twelve, thirteen, that's a lose-lose age for boys."

"And that's what you're remembering right now? All those feelings from being twelve in a boxing ring."

He shook his head. "No. Don't you get it? We weren't old enough to get into the ring. We were barely tall enough to punch the little bag. And there was nothing we could do about it but wait to grow up. And damn, that sucked!"

She put her chin on her fist, watching him with steady eyes. It took an act of will for him to stop pacing in front of her. And another surge of determination to keep himself from shaking that calm look off her face. He was twisting inside, all antsy and anxious. Like that ass of a kid he remembered.

Jesus! he thought as he abruptly dropped down onto her couch. He'd turned into that jerk of a kid, too wired to do anything but be an ass.

"What, Roger? What are you thinking?"

He threw back his head until it dropped on the back of her couch. "I'm not thinking anything, Amber. I just feel awful, okay?"

She didn't say anything, but he didn't have to look to know that she'd left her kitchen to settle down on the couch beside him. Her scent enveloped him. Her presence calmed him. Almost as much as it wound him up.

"Better be careful," he mock warned. "I'm pretty jacked up here. I'm liable to jump you." He said the words as a joke, but it wasn't far off from the truth. He was feeling ansty, nervous and angry. One of the best ways to let some of this out was to do her in the crudest, roughest way. And that really wasn't his style at all. But damn, he could throw her down, spread her legs and just pound into her.

Then he realized what he was thinking and groaned. "Holy shit, what is wrong with me?"

"Don't fight the feelings, Roger. Just feel them. Let them wash through you and go away."

"They're not going away!" he snapped. "God, this came out of nowhere! Half an hour ago, I was feeling great."

"It doesn't matter how you *were* feeling. Stay with what's going on now."

"This is why I don't go to a shrink!" He threw his hands down and glared at her. "I just feel out of control! Ansty like that jerk of a kid. Powerless like I was when I was twelve. Completely useless. Jesus. Did I tell you that Sam won't answer my emails? He says we'll talk about it when I get back. Like this fucking economy is going to wait until I get back?

I'm going to come back from vacation and there won't be a company left. Between Sam's engineering flights of fancy and the fact that most people can't afford robots, the whole place is going to crumple and there's nothing I can do about it. Just like there's nothing I can do about my goddamn blood pressure but watch it go up and up and up and ruin my goddamned life!"

He was up and pacing again, his fists planted on his hips when he wasn't gesturing wildly. And then, just like that, he stopped and took a breath. He thought back over his rant and realized, with a rather large dollop of embarrassment, that this latest screaming fit was no more rational than his explosion about the color of his cherry tomato.

"I have to get a steak," he said flatly. "All this salad has melted my brain."

She laughed, pushing up off the couch to stand directly in front of him. "It sounds like you have some control issues. And some fears about the economy."

He groaned. "Like that's original. So why am I the one on a forced vacation? Why not most of the world?"

"Because you chose high blood pressure rather than an ulcer, migraines, throat cancer or liver disease. Or whatever disease. Come on, Roger, don't worry about why you have the diagnosis. Try and release the stress that is driving you insane."

"I just need to get back to work. Sam's just being an ass—"

She stopped his words the only way she could. She kissed him, and with a lightning shift of gears, he decided he was more than amenable to the distraction. He grabbed her around the waist and pulled her right up against him. God, she felt good as he ground his hard penis against her. But then she pulled back, her eyes dark with hunger, but her expression serious.

"These feelings are real, Roger. You'll have to deal with them sometime."

"I am dealing with them," he said as he started backing her into her bedroom. "I need to bang something."

"And you want it to be me?" she asked.

"You objecting?"

She shook her head, pushing her own pelvis back enough to make him growl deep into her throat. "But after you're done banging out your frustration, you're going to have to meditate."

"Oh, God, Amber, enough with the meditation alread—"

She covered his mouth with her hand, cutting off his words if not his expression. He was done with contemplating his navel. Done with emptying his brain so that all these stupid emotions could fill them. He'd been better off when he was thinking so hard he didn't feel any of this.

Except some part of him knew it wasn't true. The part of him that wasn't consumed with rage or lust, the part of him that could find a corner of quiet in this brain. That part reminded him that he had been feeling helpless and angry for a very long time. Sure, he'd covered it with work. Hell, he'd gotten his degree in record time, then had dived straight into eighty-hour work weeks. If it weren't for his blood pressure, he'd still be at it, firmly tucking the emotions away.

God, when had the fury gotten so hot? So dark? So powerful?

It didn't matter. It was with him now. As was a hot and willing woman.

"Okay," he growled as he grabbed her wrist and pulled her hand away from his mouth. "I'll look at my *feelings*." He sneered the word. "I'll meditate, I'll think about my issues."

"You will?" she asked, her tone indicating her surprise.

"Yes," he snapped. "Now I've got one question for you."

She arched her brow.

"How do you feel about taking it from behind?" And with those words, he spun her around and bent her right in half.

13

AMBER FELT A THRILL of power rush through her at his rough handling. She knew that Roger could be the gentlest of lovers. She'd experienced that time and again this last week. But right now, he was blowing off steam. He was struggling with feeling out of control, and boy, did she understand that! After all, she was an MD who, almost by definition, liked to play God. Which meant she had her own share of dominance demons inside her. But perhaps that was why they worked so well together. She understood what he needed. And right now, that wasn't her bent over and presenting. He needed a challenge, he needed someone to fight him nose to nose and not break, even if she lost.

So while he was stripping out of his pants, she spun around to face him, her brow arched in challenge. "Been there, done that, big boy. In the elevator, or don't you remember? What else you got?"

If she had any doubt as to how he'd react, it disappeared in that moment. His hands stilled on his belt, his eyes darkened and his nostrils flared. But a slow smile began to curve his lips. Then he whipped his belt out and held it high.

"I could tie you up," he said, his voice dark with promise.

She straightened and as quick as she could manage, she

grabbed his belt and wrapped it around her arm. She could tell she surprised him, and that made them both happy.

"You could," she drawled. "Or we could just see who's the stronger bitch."

"You called me the alpha dog the day we first met." He arched a brow. "Or don't you remember that?"

She leaned forward. "I remember. I'm just demanding you prove your status. After all, who knows? Maybe all that salad has turned *everything* to mush."

He jerked backward on the belt which was still wrapped around her arm. *Bam,* she flew into his arms where he captured her tight against him. His legs were even braced apart, framing her thinner ones. And yeah, she could definitely tell that mush was *not* one of his problems. He was rock hard and pulsing with heat.

"Game on," he breathed, then he bent to plunder her mouth.

She fought him. Not to avoid his possession, but to possess *him.* While he tried to push into her mouth, she struggled to get into his. She'd never done this before with any man, but wow, this was fun. They ended up climbing over each other in their attempts to assert dominance. They lost their balance and tumbled to her futon, but that didn't break the game. It only added more of a challenge.

Then he played dirty. He'd been worming his hands underneath her shirt, so when he abruptly reared upright, her clothing went with her. Her yoga top stripped off in one piece only to catch on their entwined arms. He'd have to unwrap the belt if he wanted her shirt fully off.

Apparently he didn't because while she was gasping in shock at her sudden nakedness, he descended back onto her. This time he won the possession of her mouth, but she got something else. She got hold of his penis and gripped him tight enough to catch his attention. His pants were already open, so he had only his silk boxers to soften the strength of her hand. He stilled, then slowly straightened up from her, his eyes dark and his expression hungry.

"Here's what we're going to do," she said clearly. "You're going to get naked and let me tie you up."

His eyebrows shot to his forehead, but he didn't speak.

"And then," she continued, "you're going to lie there and take whatever I choose to dish out."

He chuckled, shaking his head no. "I don't—"

His words stopped on a strangled gasp as she gripped him even tighter. "You are going to obey me," she rasped.

"You can't hold on forever, Amber," he growled. "The minute you let go of your grip, I'm going to turn you over and spank you."

Now that did surprise her. No one had ever threatened to spank her, not even as a kid. But she found the threat rather titillating. Especially since they both knew he was bigger and stronger than her. In a fair fight, he would win hands down. Good thing she had no intention of playing fair.

Her eyes drooped and she tried to make her lip tremble. "You wouldn't use your big manly strength against me, would you? That's not fair."

He leaned right up to her nose and whispered, "Try me."

So she did. She gripped him hard enough to make his jaw bunch. And as she did, she unwound her arm from the belt. She made sure to hold his gaze the entire time, tensing for the moment he would leap. But she never wavered with her grip, never gave him the idea that she would go easy on him.

Okay, step one accomplished. Her yoga top was off. She stood before him naked from the waist up. Now on to step two: getting him naked.

"Let go of the belt."

He did, raising his hands slowly into the air.

"Now take off your shirt."

Again, he did exactly as she bid. But he didn't lure her into loosening her grip. Not even when he stood there apparently docile as she pushed his pants down to his ankles.

"Now back up and slowly lie down on the bed."

She maneuvered slowly, working hard to keep her grip strong. He was impressively large, so that helped. But it was more awkward than she'd expected, trying to hold on to a man's penis through silk while he lowered himself onto her futon. She managed it, but only barely.

And then she realized she had a problem. She had a futon without a headboard. Nothing but fabric and lightweight plastic crates. Sure, she had a belt in her free hand, but even if she could manage to wrap it around his wrists, there was nothing to anchor him to. And smart man that he was, he knew exactly what was going on.

"Problem?" he drawled.

"Of course not. I—"

He struck. She hadn't even loosened her grip, but he called her bluff. He probably guessed that she wouldn't do anything to really damage his anatomy, so he surprised her with a quick blow to her shoulders. She even saw the move coming, likely because he intended her to. He raised his hands and shoved them forward at her, and she reacted as most normal people would, raising her arms to block the blow. She succeeded, taking most of the impact on her forearms. It took a split second more for her to realize that she'd lost her grip on him.

Oops.

Especially since he continued the motion, surging up off the bed and wrapping his arms around her, restraining her movement. A second later, he used his size to push her down. Before she could take a second breath, he had her pinned beneath him. And even worse, he didn't need something like a headboard to hold her down. His larger bulk made it easy for him to keep her still while grabbing the belt.

She fought him, of course. She wriggled and pushed and even nipped at him. But it wasn't enough. He hauled her arms above her, then used the belt to cuff her wrists together. She would have slammed her arms down on top of him, but he kept his weight on them enough that she couldn't budge.

But now he was the one with the problem. She still had her yoga pants on.

"Now what you gonna do?" she taunted.

He arched a brow. "I'll make a deal with you. You take off your pants while I suit up." He indicated the box of condoms on the floor nearby. "It's a fair trade unless you want to risk pregnancy."

She stilled for a moment, her mind distracted from their game. A child. *His* child. The idea was completely nuts. She didn't have the money to support a kid right then. Not to mention that she wasn't sure she'd make a good mother. After all, shouldn't parents at least have a pretense of understanding themselves and their world? She was still floundering. She hadn't even decided if she was going back to traditional medicine and Mandolin yet.

And as she was struggling with all those thoughts, she watched Roger's eyes widen in surprise, his body stilling. Well, most of his body. His organ pulsed hard against her, telling her without words how much he was interested in making a baby with her.

But it was nuts. Completely nuts.

"Oh, my God," he whispered. "You win." Then he abruptly pulled off her, his hands shaking as he rolled to a sitting position beside her. She followed him up, her own body feeling a little weak. She had to keep her bound hands in front of her, but that didn't stop her from pressing tight to his side.

"I didn't say anything," she protested.

"You didn't have to. You were thinking about it."

She pressed a kiss into his shoulder, feeling the heat from

his skin as well as the play of muscles underneath. "It was a passing thought, Roger. I do want children someday. Maybe even yours, but—"

"I know. But we just met. You only feed me salad. It might feel like the perfect thing right now—"

"But we've known each other a week," she continued for him. "A great week, but just a week."

"You'd make a great mother," he said.

She laughed at that. "Not a prayer. I still don't know which end of my life is up. But you'd be an awesome dad."

He turned to her, pressing his lips to her forehead. "You're so patient. I've never seen anyone as honest and patient as you are. And you're brilliant, too. That's gotta help, right? Kids these days are way smarter than I ever was."

"I don't know about smarter, but definitely slicker. And thanks to the internet, they can find out a zillion dangerous and awful things. Just a few keystrokes and you can pull up a list of pranks purposely designed to drive your parents crazy."

He groaned as he pulled her into a fierce hug. "You'd still be great."

"You'd make up for my lacks. You know what you want. You could teach them so much about discipline and goal setting and how to stay focused without wandering off following every little flight of fancy that hits you."

He turned to look into her eyes. "Is that what you think you've done?"

She shrugged, feeling suddenly vulnerable. "Yeah," she finally confessed. "I often do."

"I think you're innovative and brave."

"Ha!" she snapped. "Not brave. Just really, really stubborn."

"Works for me," he said and stroked a finger down her cheek. Then he leaned forward. She met him halfway. There was no dominance struggle this time. Just the two of them sharing a tender kiss. One that steadily built in intensity. Within a moment, he was undoing the belt holding her wrists. Then as soon as she was free, she stripped off her pants while he reached for a condom. He ripped open the package, but stopped when he noticed she was watching him.

"I like the idea," he said softly. "I really do, but—"

"We're not ready. Neither of us."

He nodded slowly, and she reached over. Together they rolled the condom on.

And then he began to stroke her. Soft caresses over her face, then breasts. She was panting with desire by the time he slid a finger between her folds. She touched him, too, any and every part of his glorious body that she could reach. Then he settled between her thighs and she opened them to receive him. But he didn't enter her. Instead, he held himself still until she was looking into his eyes.

"Thank you," he whispered.

She arched her brows. "For what?"

"For showing me that life doesn't have to be a fight."

"It was a sex game," she said slowly.

"And it was great." He leaned down to stroke a tender kiss along her lips. "But this is better," he said. Then he slowly, steadily entered her.

"Way better," she whispered as she raised her legs to hold him tight.

They began to move together, their bodies in sync as never before. And it lasted long after they had both crested. In fact, Amber was still feeling it after it was done and they were curled together, relaxed as they should be after a great bout of sex. She felt safe and happy. She still had questions about her life, but in this moment, she felt strong enough to face them.

And so she straightened up enough to look at him.

"Roger," she said.

He slowly opened his eyes. "Hmm?"

"There's something I have to tell you. About Jack and our trip to Mandolin."

14

ROGER LISTENED, his heart sinking as Amber started talking about her friend at Mandolin. It got so he hated the name Jack and worried about his ability to meet the man civilly in a few days.

It wasn't so much what she said as how she said it. She started simply, telling him that her old boss—"the bastard" was finally retiring. According to Jack, if she started reconnecting with her old colleagues, started playing those political cards right, she stood a really good shot at getting her job back.

Well, he wasn't surprised. A woman as focused and talented as she was should be getting job offers left and right. Good job offers. The larger mystery was why she was sitting in Cherry Hills nursing her neighbors. And that's when the discussion got really dicey because she started talking about Jack.

"We used to have these epic battles," she said, her voice warming in memory. "Research, physics, the latest movie, it didn't matter because we always ended up in bed. It was turbulent, verging on violent, and yet—"

"You loved it," Roger said. He couldn't quite bring himself to ask if she'd loved him.

"I don't know. It was all part and parcel of that life.

Everything was a constant struggle, constant battle." She turned to face him more squarely. "You have to know that what I said about me and relationships is true. I've always been more focused on my career than on men. Jack and I were just…" She sighed. "We were buddies with benefits, and that ended a long, long time ago."

He pushed up into a sitting position, leaning his back against the cold cinder block wall. She rested on his chest, coiling her legs around his. Normally he would have been hard within a minute, then on top of her within five. But not this time. Not when he was finally getting some answers to her past. And how it had all been wrapped up in some other guy.

"But there was passion there, wasn't there?"

She sighed. "Was it passion or adrenaline addiction? Was it desire or just a caffeine habit? I'm a doctor, Roger. That's what I do, even when what I'm doing is researching energy healing. Career first, guys a very distant second."

"But you're going back there to find out, aren't you? That's why you set up the meeting with Jack, isn't it?"

She straightened. "I set up your meeting with Jack because I believe in your products and I thought RFE had something to bring to the table. And as for me and Jack, we had broken up long before I left Mandolin. I didn't even think about him when I made the decision to leave."

He believed her. But the tension in her words told him something else. "And now? Now that you're going to see him again?"

She smiled and gestured to the bed. "After this, do you really think I'd be thinking about an old boyfriend?"

He shrugged, doing his best to cover the anxiety he felt in his gut. "Maybe. Are you?"

"God, no!" she laughed. At his relieved sigh, she reached up and kissed him. Gently, but thoroughly enough that he was ready to push her back down on the futon. But she ended the kiss and pulled back. "However," she said slowly, "the meeting between you and Jack does give me a way to test the waters back at Mandolin. I'd have a reason to be there, plus the credit for bringing in a great company—yours—for a joint venture or something, and—"

"A way to look at the land. See if you could rejoin a hospital again." A hospital way out in freaking Arizona. He swallowed. "Does it have to be out there? I mean, aren't there hospitals here?"

"Yes, there are," she said as she tucked close to him again. "But there's family history there, and you know that Mandolin is a leader. Change the way Mandolin operates, and other hospitals will follow. I could possibly affect the course of Western medicine. You don't know how tempting that is."

"Of course I understand," he said, though inside, his thoughts were screaming for him to stop her. But that was selfish of him. Her career was out there. He got that. So he forced himself to act the supportive boyfriend. "What I don't really get is why you haven't gone out there before now."

"Because I like my life here. I'm doing good work."

He arched his brows, not that she could see. "Really? Serving fruit smoothies to gambling addicts and single mothers. Doing yoga and meditation in the rare moments when they leave you alone. That's not work, Amber. That's a charity vacation."

He felt her body still and knew that he had crossed a line. They'd never really talked about what she was doing in her energy "sessions," even though she did them daily for hours. She sat at a table with a manual and a pad, then spent a lot of time staring into space. As far as he could tell, she was simply writing bizarre notations and meditating.

He knew she believed the shifts in his blood pressure were due to her energy work. But he thought it had more to do with their great sex and the endless piles of salad. And now he was pushing her to see how ridiculous her new lifestyle was.

She straightened to look him in the eye. "You don't believe in anything I've been doing here," she said softly. "You think that the traditional medical model is the best, even though it's done nothing to help you."

He shifted, knowing he was treading on dangerous ground. "Hypertension is a complicated problem with multiple factors..."

She huffed. "And you don't think any of those factors could be energetic? That perhaps there's something that medicine isn't exploring because it's not linked to a drug?"

He leaned forward, trying to understand how this brilliant woman had gone from a promising medical career to spouting energetic hookum. "You put all those years into traditional medicine. Tell me you think it's all ridiculous. That a thousand years of science hasn't figured anything out."

"Of course it has!" she said, throwing up her hands. "I just don't think it's found out *everything*. There are lots of people like you who don't respond to Western therapies. I think it's because medicine isn't looking in the right places."

"But you are?"

She nodded, but the motion was less sure. "Yeah, I think I am. I think the direction I'm going in is very promising."

He looked around her apartment pointedly. She lived in a converted warehouse in a neighborhood that cops never entered except in pairs. Her clothing was stacked in plastic crates and the sum total of her worldly possessions probably wouldn't add up to her paycheck in one month of working back at her old job.

She noticed his gaze, of course. He'd meant her to. And she gaped at him. "Why would you think that money and research go hand in hand?"

"What research, Amber? You sit in a corner and stare at the wall."

"I have clients. I do work. Just because you can't see what I'm doing with your eyes doesn't mean it's not happening." She stood up and grabbed a robe from a nail on the wall. "Why are you pushing this now? Is this part of your anger from before? Is this—"

"It's not part of my..." He didn't even have a word for what he'd experienced before. "My bizzaro mood. It's about you, Amber, about what you want in your life. Why did you run here? Why did you suddenly drop everything to live in a warehouse in Chicago?"

She winced and he knew he had the right of it. Something huge had happened and whatever it was, she was still running from it. He could see she was about to turn away, about to shut him out, but he couldn't let her do that. It was too important for her to face, so that she could get on with her life. So he went to her, gripping her arms to hold her still.

"Talk to me, Amber. I can listen without judgment."

"It's not like I headed a criminal mafia or something."

"Whatever it was, whatever you want to discuss, I want to listen."

She glared at him, but he didn't waver. In the end, she gave in, though she twisted out of his arms as she did it. "I need chocolate first."

He nodded. He understood comfort food. So he followed her into the kitchen where he watched her blend up avocado, dates, blue agave syrup and cocoa powder. She didn't speak as she worked, and he let her bang about her kitchen in silence. He knew she'd get to it eventually, and sure enough she did, but only after she'd spooned her concoction into a bowl and called it chocolate mousse.

"You're kidding, right?" he said, failing in his promise to

be nonjudgmental. He just hadn't expected her to serve him brown avocado and call it mousse.

"Just taste it. Or not," she snapped. "More for me." Then she took a spoon and dug in. It should have been erotic watching her lick chocolate stuff off with all appearance of enjoyment. It would have been if he hadn't known what had gone into that stuff.

But he'd made a promise and so he felt honor bound to stick to it, even if it was about weird food. So he took a small bite and raised his eyebrows in surprise. It tasted...good. Not exactly chocolate mousse like he was used to, but like the "living food lasagna," he had to take it on its own terms. It was creamy, tasty and very chocolatey. Almost like mousse, except that it wasn't. Still, he took another bite because compared to salad, this was heaven. And as his reward, she finally began to talk.

"How long do you go down a path before you call it quits? Before you say it's wrong? Or it's not right enough for me?"

He frowned at her. "I don't do research, Amber. I'm the guy who tries to sell what the geeks produce."

"But you started out in law, right? Doesn't your résumé say law school?"

He nodded. "But I didn't want to practice law, not even business law. I really wanted to understand the legal aspects of a business and how to make them work for me instead of against me. Sure, it took some time for me to figure that out, but once I understood what I wanted I never looked back."

"But did you have some false starts? Did you look at criminal law or, I don't know—"

"Copyright law."

She raised her eyebrows. "Really?"

He nodded. "It's still pretty useful for me. Patents, intellectual rights, even privacy laws, especially as it pertains to the internet. They all relate to some small degree. I explored it, enjoyed it, even thought about having it be my career."

"And?"

He shrugged. "It didn't fit. I liked what I was doing with Sam way more than any esoteric discussion with another lawyer. Yeah, there were real-world cases. More and more as it turned out, but I like being in a business, taking Sam's creations and seeing it all the way through to a profitable market."

She pointed her spoon at him. "But what in particular made you shift away from copyright law?"

He shrugged. "Nothing in particular. It was just a series of little things that said this isn't nearly as much fun as that."

She nodded. "That's kind of how it worked for me, except that I was going between this isn't working at all and this is only working a little. Take your blood pressure, for example. Best-case scenario, you take a pill every morning for the rest of your life that keeps your blood pressure down and *bam*, we call you healthy."

He frowned. That would be healthy, in his opinion. He wouldn't have to quit his job, wouldn't have to worry about what he ate, wouldn't have to constantly wonder if the occasional throbbing in his temples was just Sam making him nuts or the precursor to a stroke.

"That's not healthy, Roger," she said softly. "That's management. Your body shouldn't need a pill to regulate its blood pressure."

"But it does."

"But it shouldn't. So you're not really healthy until your body can regulate it without medication."

He nodded. "So you're looking for a cure. Great. I'm all for it. Find out what the underlying causes for high blood pressure are and find a way to fix them. Except you can't fix DNA, you can't fight the mental factors and you can't heal everybody."

"What if we could?"

"Heal everyone?"

She shrugged. "What if there's a whole new way to look at your physical body as vibrations and atoms and—"

"Physics and electricity?"

She nodded.

"Now you're sounding like Sam."

She smiled. "I knew there was a reason I liked RFE."

"But if that's the case, then you should be working in bio-engineering, consulting with us, or I don't know—"

"Doing research in the direction that I think medicine should go?"

"Yes!"

She looked at him hard. "I already am."

He sighed. "With your notebook and your paper and your navel gazing?"

She straightened up from the counter and started packing away the chocolate. She didn't speak until her back was to him. "Do you tell Sam what to do when he starts inventing something?"

Roger snorted. "All the time."

"And does he listen?"

"Sometimes. Well, only a little of the time. Well, maybe never."

She turned around to stare at him. "Then why do you think you know better than I do how to do my research?"

He winced. She had a point. "But come on, Amber. Meditation has its place. But it's not going to cure cancer."

She arched her brow. "You know that for sure? What's the latest research on cancer patients who meditate?"

He didn't know. He hadn't a clue if that was even an area of study. "Fine," he said. "I'm wrong about trying to direct your research. You're the MD. You know what you're doing way better than I do."

"Thank you."

"But you could have done that at Mandolin. You could have cut back your hours and stared at the wall there. You didn't have to give up everything and run here to nowheresville Chicago. So what happened, Amber? Why did you leave?"

She sighed and said the one thing he'd feared from the very beginning. "I killed a patient."

15

AMBER STRUGGLED WITH the emotions clogging her throat. It was hard enough for her to face what had happened two years ago—she sure as hell didn't want to do it now in front of Roger. But she knew that if he hadn't forced this discussion on her, she might never face it. So she girded herself, so to speak, and tried to explain to herself as well as him about what had happened back then.

"Her name was Vera Barker. She was my boss's patient, but she came to me with questions. She was so weak from chemo and she wanted advice on alternative treatments."

He nodded. "So you gave her some suggestions."

"Yeah. Nothing drastic. Just diet changes, energy sessions and the like. And it worked. She was getting stronger and healthier every day."

"That's good, right? That's not killing her. That's kinda the opposite."

Amber smiled, but the gesture was weak. "Well, my boss saw that she was getting stronger, and since he was going on vacation soon, he upped the timing of her radiation treatments."

"Oh, hell," he whispered.

"She was stronger, but not that strong. In the end, she had a heart attack and died."

"I'm so sorry, Amber. That must have been awful. But I still don't see how that's you killing the patient."

She shrugged. "It's not really. But I have come to realize that I did play a part in her death."

He frowned at her. "What? I don't understand."

"I didn't tell my boss about it. So, according to the administration, I went behind another doctor's back, prescribed something *not* approved by the AMA, and as a result, the patient died."

Roger pulled back and folded his arms across his chest. "You've got to be kidding me."

She shook her head. "Look, it's not as cut and dried as it sounds. Hospitals have rules, and I broke a cardinal one. Two actually, prescribing stuff behind another doctor's back and suggesting that New Age stuff had any value at all. Mandolin has a very hard line against both of those."

"So you got in trouble and left." She could see the pieces fall into place in his mind. "But you think that they'll take you back now?"

She hedged. "I don't know. According to Jack, my boss has done some more boneheaded things. The director has seen how much of an idiot the guy is, and I could probably spin my previous case as being a victim of his manipulations."

"I don't see that as spin, Amber."

"Yeah, maybe. But Bob wasn't the only narrow mind there." She lifted her hand, then began ticking off thoughts on her fingers. "Pros for going back to Mandolin. I'd be near my family again, I'd make a decent living, I could see a ton more patients than I can as I'm working now, and potentially, I'd be helping to shift the course of American medicine. At a minimum, I would add to the debate of holistic versus traditional medicine."

"All good things."

She nodded. "Now the cons. I'd be returning to big-company politics, I don't know that I'd be accepted, and I don't know if I can toe the line if the narrow minds are still in charge."

"Sounds like you need to go back there and find out."

She sighed. "Yeah. It does." But what if she found out she wanted to return? One week ago, that would have been a miracle. She'd stop being at odds with her family, she'd have a bank account again and she would have a place to work that was exciting, dynamic and important. But one week ago, she hadn't known Roger. And now she wasn't at all sure she could give him up.

She was still looking for a way to answer when she felt his arms wrap around her. She hadn't been expecting his touch, hadn't even heard him shift on the futon. But then she felt his arms around her belly, slowly urging her to lean back against him. She couldn't stop herself. She relaxed into him. Then he spoke, his lips right next to her temple.

"It's okay to admit that you want to go back. It's okay to say you miss your old life."

She started, twisting around to look at him. "But that's the point. I'm not sure I do."

His expression turned tender, though his eyes verged on tortured. "Really? Except wasn't that how our whole relationship started? You missed sex with the alpha dog."

"God, I am never going to live that down!" she cried.

"But it's true! You missed that whole high-powered life-style. Enough to dress up for me and get me going in an elevator."

She pushed to her feet, amazed at how he could focus on one thing—one single event—and draw so many wrong conclusions.

"And what since then has led you to think I want to go back

to that? The fact that I parade around in my stiletto boots?" She pointed to her bare feet. "The fact that I'm begging you to take me to high-end restaurants and we're spending so much time in your expensive apartment playing with your expensive toys?" In fact, she hated spending the night at his place. He still had too much clutter in his life. "Or what about the fact that I've been pushing you to get aggressive with your blood pressure by getting echocardiograms and DNA analysis and whatever else modern medicine has devised to explore hypertension?" She'd suggested exactly none of that. "Roger, why would you think I want any of that again?"

"Well," he said, defeat in every note of his voice. "Mostly because you're not telling me to go to hell."

"Go to hell, Roger."

He straightened. "Because you started this as a confession—your word, not mine."

She threw up her hands. "Roger. Quit playing with words."

"And finally, the fact that I was curious about what your energy sessions were. I wanted to know more about what you were doing when you stare into space at your desk. And what I found instead right on top was your brand-new résumé. And beside that a series of notes on how to explain what you'd been doing for the last two years. Everything from mental breakdown to a scientific exploration of alternative medicines that ultimately proved useless."

She blanched. She actually felt the blood drain from her face. "I was exploring, Roger. Making notes on what I would have to say and do to go back there."

"And what did it tell you?"

"Nothing!" she shot back. "They were just notes."

He shrugged. "Maybe. And maybe they're you testing out whether you want to go back or not. Whether your vacation in the slums has done its job. Amber, we're arguing an awful lot here, and I'm not even sure what about. You just seem angry to me. And confused. And maybe a little lost."

She stared at him, her mind reeling. She was doing a lot of yelling and a lot of accusing. She had started this conversation as a confession, but what had she meant by that? Had she really meant that she was going back to Mandolin? Maybe for real?

"Oh, hell." She ended up collapsing back onto the futon. "I have no idea what I want."

"That's okay," he said, his voice depressed even as he gathered her into his arms. "We'll figure it out together."

HOURS LATER, Roger had cause to regret his words. They had spent hours discussing and analyzing and arguing about everything from national health-care policies to the idiocy of having a "buddy with benefits." He'd learned more about how hospitals *really* worked than he'd ever wanted to know. And worse, he learned that Amber was not only driven and smart, but she was *smart*. As in genius-level brilliant.

He'd assumed that she spent her days much as they had in the last week: reading, relaxing and eating salad. Sure, there was some internet time for her, energy sessions at her desk and of course their marathon sex-capades, for which he was eternally grateful. But he never suspected that their time together had been as much a vacation for her as it had been for him.

So what did she really spend her time on? Exactly what she'd said at the beginning: research into alternate holistic health practices. She was certified in a number of modalities including acupuncture, healing hands and qigong. What was she exploring right now? Something called energy mirrors which she said was extremely promising.

If he thought she was wasting her time before he learned all this, now he was even more convinced that she was underutilized. Not because of what she was exploring—he didn't understand half of it. But because she deserved to have a team of experts working with her, compiling data, analyzing possibilities, assisting her research the way it could be done with a pile of money. In truth, it was the kind of team that Mandolin was known for. Except, of course, it was not traditional medicine and Amber wondered if she'd get the people in charge to hear what she'd discovered, much less put money behind it.

He had no idea what to think one way or the other. Hospital politics were not even close to his area of expertise, much less the astrophysics or ancient Chinese philosophy that she rattled off with such ease. In this, at least, she reminded him of Sam at his most brilliant. They both would just talk and point and do while everyone around them scrambled to keep up. Roger had given up trying to compete on that intellectual level a long time ago.

Which meant that he had to go with what he knew for sure. First, Amber was brilliant and he could stop trying to tell her what to think. She was well beyond him in that department. Second, he might not have any faith in ancient Chinese secrets or water isotopes that bonded with bad juju, but he absolutely believed in her. All he had to do was follow her suggestions—even if it meant eating chocolate mousse made out of avocado—and he'd end up okay. Or if not okay, at least better than he'd been before. Hell, he'd been on this diet for just over a week and he felt better, thought more clearly and was generally more calm than ever before.

Third and most frightening of all, he realized he was starting to fall for her. The feeling had been creeping up on him for a while now. At first, he'd just thought it was the endlessly wonderful times in bed with her. What man didn't want a woman just as addicted to sex as he was? But tonight, he'd realized it was more than that.

He adored the way she thought. Her mind wandered in endless ways he couldn't always follow, but were always interesting. She listened to him—really listened—and had no problem challenging his logic or conceding to him when he was right.

Then there was the final blow, so to speak. The way he was when he was with her. He hadn't noticed it at first. Of course he felt calmer when he was around her. He was on vacation. But he'd never felt this peaceful with anyone, vacation or not. Worse, she challenged him in subtle ways. She never pushed, well, not hard. But he found himself working to be better because of her.

He wanted to be more patient and a better listener. He wanted to eat bizarre foods, just because it made her happy. He wanted to stay beside her every day of her life just so he could see what she discovered along the way. And she would discover things, because how could she not? She had all the pieces. She just had to have the support—financially and emotionally.

Which left him with two inescapable conclusions. The first was inevitable, given the mountain of evidence. He was falling head over heels in love, and he would do just about anything to stay by her side.

And the second? That she was destined for far bigger things than a converted warehouse in Chicago and marriage to a guy who knew enough to surround himself with geniuses but wasn't one himself. In short, he was doomed. And the minute she stepped back into that life—at the Mandolin in a few days or with whatever huge research grant came her way—Amber would fly on to greener pastures and better men. And he would be left alone with an empty bowl of salad and a broken heart.

16

AMBER WAS SURPRISED to discover that the flight to Phoenix was beyond delightful. She had cleared Roger to go back to RFE two days earlier, provided that he stuck to his living-food diet. He'd agreed, though there were a few grumbles about how his reputation would suffer the moment everyone saw him eating rabbit food.

Always before, her flights had been filled with work. Two years ago, her BlackBerry had never been off except for during takeoff and landing. At which point, she'd pull out articles she ought to read, and paperwork that absolutely had to be done.

This time, she was flying without any work beyond a novel she wanted to read. Her job was to grease the connection between Mandolin and RFE. And if she spent a lot of time looking and wondering if she could fit back into the good parts of her old life without dragging in the bad, well, that didn't take any preparation. That just took open eyes and ears.

What she hadn't expected was how absolutely fabulous it was to talk to Sam. Sure, she'd known he was the genius inventor side of RFE, but she hadn't realized how delightful it was to explore the way a brilliant engineer thought. His brain was quirky. There was no other way to describe it. Downright quirky in how it leaped from one thing to the next without any obvious pattern except for brilliance. He saw connections that no one else did. And for the first time in a very long time, she sensed a kindred spirit. Someone who thought sideways and had to work to understand normal people.

It was wonderful. She spent the trip talking with him about his latest projects, what he'd just seen on television the day before, his upcoming wedding in a week. Anything and everything was up for grabs, and by the end of the flight she was both energized and completely exhausted.

Right here was a clue as to why she and Jack had never made their relationship work. She'd had this kind of connection with him as well—two lateral-thinking brains spinning off of each other—but after a couple hours, it was exhausting. Her brain just needed to shut up. But she seemed incapable of stopping. At the luggage carousel, she and Sam talked airport design. In the cab ride to their hotel, they talked the ergonomics of car seats. And in the lobby as they were checking in, they started to discuss global warming. Sweet heaven, she was never more thrilled than when she finally waved good-bye to Sam at his hotel room and crossed to the peace of her room with Roger.

Oddly enough, he had been very quiet during the whole trip. She'd tried to include him in the discussions, but he hadn't tried to keep up. Every once in a while he'd throw in something pithy, but generally he let her and Sam spin while he listened with a more and more morose expression.

And now, as she dropped backward onto their king-sized bed, she was able to close her eyes for a moment and cherish the quiet. Blessed quiet. For about three seconds. Her mind was still spinning, her thoughts whirling with possible this and what they'd said about that.

Which meant she had two choices for shutting up her brain. She could meditate it away, sitting in silence and letting all the noise bleed off of her. The habit was well installed and just thinking about it helped quiet the most neurotic corners of her brain. Or she could descend into a very wonderful, thoroughly satisfying round of mutual pleasure with Roger. The second option was much more appealing. Their meeting with Jack wasn't until tomorrow and they could always order in-room dining. Which meant, they'd have all night long to play if they wanted.

So with her best come-hither look, she rolled onto her side and smiled at her companion. "Hey, studly," she drawled.

He had his back to her as he set up his laptop, but at her words, she saw his whole body still. He managed one more click of the mouse before turning to her.

She was about to say something obvious like, "Did you bring the handcuffs?" But at the expression on his face, she held back the sexual banter. His face was tight, his body held stiffly. Obviously something was on his mind, so she pushed upright on the bed and faced him square on.

"So, you've been awful quiet."

He shrugged. "I didn't have anything to add."

She would have laughed if he didn't seem so serious. "You always have something to add. And usually it's something about staying on topic and following a thought to its logical end."

He arched a brow. "I don't mean to stifle your creativity."

This time she did laugh. "Creativity is as much about discipline as it is about thinking bizarrely, and so you have told me time and time again."

He sighed, spinning his chair around to fully face her. "You know, we've been together for barely two weeks. I'm not sure we can have a time and time again."

She frowned, wariness chilling her heart. "What exactly are you saying, Roger?"

"Just that we've only known each other a couple of weeks. Nothing more."

She might have believed him. His voice sounded sincere. Even his body position was steady, if not exactly open, but his gaze didn't quite meet hers. So she scrambled off the bed and touched his face, forcing his eyes up to hers.

"Why is everything weird all of a sudden?" she asked.

He huffed. "It's not weird—"

"God, don't lie to my face. Just tell me. Do you want me to get a separate room? Is it hard to be here working and yet with me? Have you suddenly realized that I talk way too much?"

He pressed his fingers to her lips, and a reassuring smile curved his lips. "Stop! Geez, Amber, it's just a—"

"Don't say 'mood.' With one notable exception, you don't have moods. And even that one had a reason. So tell me the truth, Roger. What's going on in that very busy brain of yours?"

His mouth opened on a short gasp of surprise. "My brain is busy? *My* brain? Did you listen to you and Sam? Good Lord, Einstein couldn't have kept up with you two."

She swallowed. "Einstein would have left us in the dust. Have you ever tried to read his *Theory of Relativity?* I'm good at math, but that stuff left me clueless by page six."

"Page six, huh? Well, I guess you're just a slacker there." He pressed a long, tender kiss to her lips. She would have made it deeper, would have pushed for more intimacy, but he ended it and slowly straightened. "Most of us don't get beyond page two."

She looked up at him. "You've tried to read it?"

He nodded. "Sam called me stupid once when we were ten. So I challenged him to a contest. We'd both study something that was incredibly complicated to see if the other could understand it and apply it to the world today. He picked Einstein's theory."

She smiled, impressed once again by him. What ten-year-old tried to fathom the *Theory of Relativity?* "So who won the bet?"

Roger laughed. "Neither of us. Sam at least made it to page four, though."

"Roger, I was still playing with my Barbies at ten."

"And scrubbing in on veterinary surgeries, if I recall."

Oh, yeah. She had told him that. "Well, that was because I was lucky and my uncle had a soft spot for little girls."

"Brilliant little girls."

"Pot calling the kettle black."

He huffed, his shoulders slumping with the sound. "Amber, look, let's not mince words here. I'm smarter than the average guy. And I've got some pretty awesome leadership skills. Have to if I want to corral the brain trust that Sam has gathered. But that doesn't mean I'm one of you."

She blinked. "One of us?"

"An Einstein."

A few years ago, she would have demurred. She would have laughed and pooh-poohed his statement out of modesty. But it was false modesty because, honestly, she did know she was crazy smart. It wasn't exactly a secret. But that kind of brilliance didn't translate well to life skills. She'd melted down but good a few years back. In truth, she often wondered if her medical knowledge put more blocks on her thinking than actually helped.

But how did she say all that to Roger? How did she express something she was only now beginning to understand?

"You hold your own just fine," she said as she pressed her lips to his. Then she pulled back to look right into his eyes. "We need you to keep us focused. Without you, Sam would have run RFE into the ground years ago."

He nodded, accepting the statement as the fact it was. "But that's at work with my best friend," he said. "What about in a relationship? With a girl whose brain is beyond incredible?"

She smiled, slowly straightening against him so that he could feel every bump and curve on her body. "She wants you, too," she said.

That was all the encouragement he needed. His hands were on her waist, caressing the flesh there before he stripped her shirt off. She worked equally quickly, pulling off his clothes as fast as her fingers could work. But once they were naked, she slowed down. She tried to show him in words just what she thought of him. Of course, that meant she had to understand her feelings first.

She loved the way he felt beneath her fingertips, all sinuous muscle and broad masculine planes. She loved the way he took time with her body, stroking her skin, sucking her breasts, and making sure she was ready for him before he filled her.

She loved that she could talk to him about acupuncture, chakras and all sorts of weird stuff without ridicule. He didn't believe in any of it, but he listened and he told her clearly—without mocking—when she stepped off the logic train.

And best of all, she loved that she could be quiet with him. She felt grounded around him. As if he were her safety net when the scary in her life got too much to handle. He was there to catch her, to talk to her, to keep her sane.

She loved that about him. But was that love? Did she *love* him? Maybe. Or maybe not. Maybe this was just endorphins and sexual arousal from a really, really skilled lover.

She arched her back as she felt the way he expanded her, thrusting into her body with absolute skill. Her legs tightened around him, urging him deeper, stronger. He accommodated her, his breath coming out in hard gasps as he filled her again and again.

But he didn't come. He didn't drop over the edge until she went first. And she did that with a sudden ripple that became a wave. Pleasure rolled through her, and only then did she feel him surrender to his own.

Bliss. Absolute bliss.

But was it love?

She was still searching for an answer when her phone rang.

17

"It's Jack," she said, and Roger did his best not to say something he'd regret.

They were just enjoying some very intimate afterglow. It was on the tip of his tongue to confess that he was falling in love. Yes, him, the man his entire office thought was gay, was finally opening his heart to a woman. And who should interrupt? Her former lover.

Great.

"I better take it," she said just before she popped open her cell. "He might be trying to reschedule."

Roger nodded against her back, doing his best not to feel his world slipping away. How had she come to be so important to him in two weeks? Just two short weeks, and he didn't care about his damn blood pressure or this meeting that could very well be the answer to RFE staying in business. He didn't care. He just wanted her in his arms and beside him for the rest of his life.

But that was just crazy. It was like one of Sam's flights of engineering fancy when he suddenly started spouting about some idea he'd had while showering and how it was going to revolutionize the world. Roger was always the one who said hold on. Test the waters. Create the prototype and see about financing. Saving the world could come after he made payroll.

And so he said that to himself. *Hold on. See if she's moving back to Arizona and Mandolin before you start talking forever. See if you can make it a month before you go shopping for diamonds. And most important, see how she reacts to Jack's dinner invitation.* Because he could hear her phone clearly enough to know that that was exactly what her former lover wanted right then. Dinner and drinks. The bedsheet mambo was implied.

The bastard.

"I'm going to meet him for a few drinks, Roger. He wants to reconnect, talk about stuff, see what I think of RFE without you there trying the hard sell."

"Of course," Roger said, because that's what reasonable, sane guys did. "Sounds like a good idea. I'll just grab some food with Sam. Maybe work on our presentation."

"Thanks, sweetie. You're the best."

Yeah, he was the best. The best damned schmuck in Arizona and Illinois combined. He waited, watching with every appearance of calm as she slipped into a dress and those damned stiletto boots. Flirty makeup, a smart twist and her hair was up in a statuesque bun, grab the purse and give him a quick, careful kiss so as not to smudge her lipstick. Ten minutes after getting the phone call, Amber was out the door.

He waited, listening like the loser he was as her heels clicked down the hallway and the elevator dinged. Two minutes after that he got sick of his own morose thoughts, so he rolled over, grabbed his cell and dialed Sam. "You hungry?" he growled into the phone. "I'm sick of rabbit food. I want a damned steak."

JACK HADN'T CHANGED. Dark, swarthy skin, perfectly cut waves of black hair, and those eyes. Damn, he was handsome, thought Amber with a smile. And he was also on the move.

He was waiting at the bar for her, leaning back in a casual pose as he watched the ebb and flow of the people in the restaurant. It wasn't that he expected anyone except her, but several of the movers and shakers of the medical world were known to drink and dine here. It was only prudent to keep an eye open for the happy chance of running into someone who needed to know about your latest medical success.

She remembered doing exactly the same thing when she lived here. And she remembered the first time she went out to dinner in Chicago and didn't even attempt to notice anyone around her except her sister who had come out for a visit. She had felt free for the first time in years. As if the simple act of eating without keeping an eye out for a career opportunity had dropped shackles from her feet. And now here she was, stepping back into the cuffs. At that moment, Jack stood up to talk to someone at a nearby table. Amber saw who it was and stepped forward, sliding into the old meet-and-greet pattern of a mover and shaker.

"There you are, Jack! Hope I didn't keep you waiting long," she said as she easily sidestepped a chair to cross to his side.

Jack turned with his trademark smile. Half sex god, half exotic South American, it had charmed the hearts of women throughout the country. Which was especially funny since he'd been born and raised in Southern California and was the son of two lawyers. Latin American he was not. Latin lover, on the other hand...

"Amber! My God, look how beautiful you are! Whatever you've been researching it's done miracles for you. You practically glow!"

She kissed him on both cheeks as was their custom. He caressed her arm the way he'd always, with warmth, the right amount of pressure, and then an added little brush of a fingertip at the end.

"I cannot lie," she said, loud enough for the people at the table to hear her. "I have found some unexpected benefits to my research. My skin has never been this clear, my hair stopped going gray—"

"Stopped going gray? Really?" The question came from a dark-haired woman in her fifties with bright curious eyes and the wrinkles around them that were typical in one her age.

"Yes," Amber responded, her manner easy, breezy, and just perfect for an "accidental" run-in with someone important. "I actually had my hair shift from gray to brown again. It was quite the surprise."

"Oh, where are my manners?" Jack interposed smoothly. "Everyone, this is Dr. Amber Smithson, a brilliant mind that I'm trying to seduce back to Mandolin. Amber, please let me introduce…"

And they were off and running. The feeling was so strong, Amber would swear she heard the starting whistle as she stepped smoothly back into the rat race. Within moments, she and Jack were joining two members of the Mandolin board of directors for drinks. Fine wine flowed easily as did the conversation. She began munching on high-priced potato skins while arguing liver functions. Before long, someone was ordering crab cake appetizers. She ate her first cooked food in nearly two years and didn't even realize it until she'd finished the cake.

As was typical in one of these impromptu meetings, conversation wandered, but always with an agenda. Jack clearly meant to spin her two years away as scientific research in the tradition of Dian Fossey going to live with the gorillas. She'd immersed herself in the weird half-truths of holistic medicines to emerge victorious. And didn't Mandolin desperately need a woman who could credibly speak to patients about all the nonsense that was out there?

The directors listened, of course, because everyone listened to Jack. He was that mesmerizing. And then they responded with their agenda, asking pointed questions about how her résumé could build up the clinic's reputation and revenue stream.

She answered as diplomatically as she could, spinning her years away in much the same way Jack had. Research, blah, blah. Interesting anecdote. Exciting possibilities of a focused study, etc, etc.

It was very well played on everyone's part. A game she'd learned from the cradle, and as usual, Jack was as smooth a partner as one could ever wish. But by the time their new friends headed out, Amber had a headache that started at the top of her head and clenched her muscles down through her lower back.

"Well, that went perfectly, don't you think?" asked Jack as he topped off her glass of wine despite her negative shake of the head. "A few more evenings like that, and they'll be begging to take you back."

"How'd you know they'd be here?"

He grinned. "Dr. Cordon's assistant has a weakness for a certain type of ganache."

Of course she did. And of course Jack would know of it. "Just imagine," she drawled, "how much you could accomplish if you put all of your effort into helping your patients instead of splitting your focus between ganache and crab cakes."

He laughed, as this was an old argument between them. "Doctors who only worry about patients don't get research dollars."

It was a simplistic answer, but one that held more than a grain of truth. Like any high-dollar field, politics always played a roll. The field didn't matter—medicine, oil fields or baseball diamonds—who you schmoozed made a difference.

And that made Amber angry. Perhaps it always had, but just like Jack, she had accepted it as the price of modern science. But for some reason, that irritated her more than usual. Perhaps it was her pounding headache or maybe the stress of smiling and spinning and drinking again. Whatever the reason, she wasn't willing to pay the price right now. She just wanted to get back to Roger.

"Thank you, Jack," she said as she pushed to her feet.

"My pleasure, *cara*," he said, the endearment rolling off his tongue. Once that word had been a signal for more. Buddies with benefits. But not tonight. And obviously never again because the word and the caress just left her flat.

"I think it's time I got back to my hotel," she said as she stepped away.

He frowned, obviously surprised by her lack of reaction. "But Amber, we have so much more to discuss. The top people have changed. If you're coming back, you need to know who is who and what they want."

She bit her lip, torn between the career possibilities in front of her, and the desire to snuggle tight against Roger and let her headache melt away. But she was an adult, not an adolescent girl. And she had a decision to make. So with a sigh, she sat back down. "All right," she said firmly. "Hit me with it all. Who's here, who's not and what do they think about alternative therapies."

Two hours later, her head was pounding, she felt sick from the food she'd been snacking on and her mind was exploding with names and strategies for maneuvering back into Mandolin. Jack had wanted to talk longer. Lord, knowing him, they would have sat there all night. But she couldn't. After two years of silence inside her loft, even this quiet bar was too much for her. So she pushed back from the table with clear resolve.

"I'm done for tonight, Jack."

He stood up from his seat. "So soon? But it's not even ten."

She laughed, the sound strained. How had she forgotten the late hours they used to keep? Back home, ten was almost bedtime. Here? It was barely getting started.

"Big day tomorrow," she quipped, as she kissed his cheek. "Meeting with a hotshot neurosurgeon."

"Damn right you are!" Jack shot back with a grin. Then he tried to pull her into a different kind of kiss. She backed away double time. Whatever questions she had about her future, they didn't include Jack.

"Good night," she said firmly as his face fell.

"Good night, *cara*," he finally answered. She barely heard him. She was already halfway out the door.

She was in a cab, nearly back to the hotel when she got the call. It was Sam, his voice tight with panic. And he said the words guaranteed to make her reconsider her lack of credentials at the clinic.

"Amber! You've got to come to the hospital right now. Roger's collapsed!"

18

"I DIDN'T COLLAPSE," Roger grumbled as he glared at his best friend. "I just stumbled a bit."

"And went down face-first in my mashed potatoes."

Roger huffed and rubbed his hand over his face again. God, he wanted a shower, not to be sitting here in Emergency when he knew he was perfectly fine. But, of course, he wasn't perfectly fine all the time. Like when he had stood up to go to the salad bar and had abruptly lost his vision. Hence the face-plant in Sam's mashed potatoes. He felt fine now but he was sitting in an E.R. cubicle while Sam made way too big a deal out of something that he prayed was really nothing.

Problem was, after years of being told he was one stressful moment away from a coronary, he was terribly afraid that his time had just run out. And so he sat and tried not to think of worst-case scenarios while Sam paced circles around his bed. The man had just finished detailing everything to Amber— and he did mean everything, mashed potatoes and all—when he abruptly stopped, said a heartfelt thanks, then snapped his phone shut.

"Amber's on her way," Sam said.

"You're not supposed to have a cell phone on in the hospital. Interferes with the equipment or something."

Sam arched his brow. "Lousy shielding, much? Hey, maybe that's something RFE could—"

"Sam! Just shut up, will you? For once in your brilliant life, just…be quiet."

His friend sobered immediately, but his brow deepened further into a frown. Eventually, the man just couldn't take it anymore and started running at the mouth again. "I thought you were doing better. I mean, you seemed happy. Got that great sex vibe going, you know?"

Roger gave his friend a look. "Sex vibe? The sixties just called. They want their lingo back."

Sam rolled his eyes. "You know what I mean. You seemed calmer since your vacation. Less urgent about everything. I thought you were *better.*"

"I was better. I mean, I *am* better," Roger groused. "Mashed potatoes aside, I feel great."

Sam opened his mouth to speak, but a firm female voice interrupted, "People in the peak of health don't usually nose-dive into their food, Mr. Martell."

The voice was followed by an efficient brunette in low heels and tight braids that crisscrossed over her head. She looked to be somewhere in her late twenties, but could have been forty with a good plastic surgeon. And she just felt like one of those people who would have a good plastic surgeon.

"Um, hello?" he said as he read the name on her tag "Dr.—"

"Dr. Alexandra Hamilton, but you can call me a founding father." She barely paused to indicate that was a joke as she surveyed his chart. "You're not healthy, Mr. Martell, you are in fact teetering on the edge of disaster. Fortunately, we've got a crack team here and after a few tests we'll be ready to tweak you right back to your three-martini lunches."

"I don't drink martinis. Don't like them."

She looked up from her chart, her eyebrows raised

in a frozen kind of disbelief. "It's a figure of speech, Mr. Martell."

Actually, it was a kind of stereotyping that always annoyed him. People assumed because he was a certain size and had a certain type of job, that his high blood pressure was due to a lack of exercise, regular steak, and those martini lunches. But that wasn't him, and he'd like his doctor to know that. But he never got the chance. Dr. Hamilton just bowled right over him.

"I'm going to order a few tests," she said as she made some notations in his chart. "And then we'll have you back to your mashed potatoes in no time." Then she walked out. Simply walked out, though they could hear her giving orders to the nurse just outside the curtain.

Sam and Roger exchanged annoyed glances, but neither of them dared to say anything for fear of interrupting. And how ridiculous was that? They were both high-powered people, men assured of their own competence, and yet neither of them dared to say boo because it would interfere with the flow of medicine. The doctor had come in, said a few things, then just as quickly disappeared. It was how health care worked, and both men trusted that they would know something when there was something to know. Just because one doctor was a bit snooty did not mean that she was wrong.

So they sat. Or, rather, Roger sat while Sam paced. And they both prayed in their own way. In Roger's case, that meant he tried to find that meditative place of stillness and space that he had been working on with Amber. In Sam's case, it meant that the man slipped into engineering mode, staring at cables and analyzing equipment, babbling the whole time. Or he would have if Roger didn't glare him into silence.

Thankfully, the nurse came in a few minutes later and explained what had just happened. The doctor had ordered a battery of tests and would return later with a diagnosis. But for the moment, they just had to be patient.

Ten minutes later, he was giving blood. A lot of blood. Ten minutes after that, he was put in a wheelchair and whisked away for something else. All very efficient, all very frightening. More than once, Roger worried that the stress was going to touch off the stroke that everyone feared.

And where the hell was Amber? Rushing over here, he was sure. But what if in her haste she had a car accident? What if she wasn't allowed in the back to see him? She didn't have privileges at this hospital. Not anymore. Maybe she wouldn't be allowed…

Almost as if she had spoken in his head, he heard the words, *"Stop thinking!"* There was a lot more that came after that. *Be in the* now. *Focus on your breath. Pretend you are listening at the door of sick child. Let everything go quiet and listen.* All of that rolled through his brain, but sadly it didn't stop his thinking.

So he forced himself. With an act of will, he shut up his brain. He let everything that was happening just happen. He was in a hospital, after all. Whatever was going on with his body, this was the perfect place for him to be in case something terrible was happening. And so, he needed to just stop thinking. Just. Be. Quiet.

That got him through the EKG. Well, trying to keep not thinking passed the time during the test. If he were honest, he'd only been mentally quiet for a fraction of the time. Didn't matter. He wasn't worrying nearly so much. And he knew that Amber was waiting for him downstairs as soon as he was finished here.

Except, she wasn't. Sam was, and his expression was more relaxed than it had been a half hour ago.

"Sam?"

"Amber's here. She took a look at your chart, asked me

some questions and said she'd be right back. But she's here. And she told me not to worry because she was pretty sure that everything's fine."

Roger exhaled in relief. She hadn't gotten into an accident. She hadn't run off with Jack. She was here. And he was ten times more anxious to see her and a zillion times more relaxed at the same time.

Then Sam took a step forward, his manner indicating that he was imparting a great secret. "In fact, she said that she thought you were getting better. That this is just a glitch because your medication's wrong."

Roger frowned. "I've been taking this medication for years."

"But it's too much now," said Amber as she rushed around the curtain to his side, "given the changes we've been working on."

God, she looked beautiful. Even with her hair frazzled and her makeup smeared, she was the most beautiful sight in the world. Roger reached out and grabbed her hand only to have it collide with her chest as she leaned down to kiss him. If he'd had more presence of mind, he would have shifted his grip to give her an inappropriate squeeze. As it was, he simply allowed himself to relax into the glory that was all Amber.

"Ah, I believe the picture is getting clearer," said Dr. So-Not-A-Founding-Anything Hamilton. Her voice was cool, professional, and yet still managed to convey a subtle superiority. "Let me guess. This relationship is about two, maybe three weeks old?"

Amber stiffened and Roger sighed. He couldn't concentrate on the incredibly wonderful, reassuring and delightful fact that Amber was here. Not with Sam, a nurse, and Dr. Interrupting Hamilton right there. So he simply reached out with his free hand to entwine his fingers with Amber's. While she, in turn, slipped into doctor mode by extending her right hand.

"Hello. I'm Dr. Amber Smithson."

"Hello." The woman shook Amber's hand, but without any apparent warmth or interest. And the minute she let go of Amber's hand, her attention centered back on Roger. "Well, Mr. Martell," she said as she again pulled out his chart and began making notes. "It appears that you've been having a lot of fun recently. Did you just get back from a vacation with a new girlfriend?"

Roger nodded slowly, simultaneously pissed off by her condescending tone but also impressed that she got it right. "Yes, I just went back to work a couple days ago."

Dr. Hamilton nodded. "Well, I'll spare you the technical jargon and put it in layman's terms. You need to lay off the, um, couple's recreation for a little bit. Not completely—say once a week should be fine—until your blood pressure stabilizes. Then you can slowly ease back into moderate relations."

"What? You're kidding, right?" Amber cut in, shock in every line of her body. "He's overmedicated. His blood pressure was too low. That's why he fainted. He needs to cut back on his meds."

Dr. Hamilton lifted her gaze out of the chart to stare coldly back at Amber. Then she abruptly smiled...at Roger. When she spoke, her voice was crisp, efficient and cut like a chilled razor. "There are excellent reasons why doctors don't treat their loved ones, Mr. Martell. Emotions tend to cloud judgment. So you can understand, I'll explain my prescription to you. Sex tends to lower blood pressure in men. In some cases, a lot of sex..." Her voice trailed away and right on cue, Roger picked up the sentence.

"Tends to lower it a lot." And why had he done that? He didn't even like this woman, and yet the way she addressed him, plus the authority of her position as a doctor, made him settle right into the flow of her words.

"Exactly." Her expression warmed as if he was a good student.

"But that's a good thing."

"Of course it is. Until the sex slows down."

Amber spoke up, her voice excruciatingly dry. "Which is what you just prescribed. It's like you want to keep him on medication."

"I do," returned the doctor with her first show of true feeling. "It's the responsible course. His blood pressure was under control that way."

No, actually it hadn't been. That's how this whole thing had started: with a doctor telling him to quit his job or he'd have a stroke. But he didn't get a chance to say that because Amber was stepping forward.

"But he's getting better. His pressure is lower, so lower his medication."

The woman took a deep breath, but continued to speak at Roger. Apparently, she didn't even want to acknowledge Amber. "You're back at work now. The stress will come back, your—uh—stress relief will slow down because you don't have the time, and then your blood pressure will go back up. If your medication isn't at the usual level, then you risk an event that neither of us want."

The way she said "event" brought up every nightmare that haunted Roger. His father drooling on himself in the treatment facility after his stroke, the funerals of his uncle and grandfather, every family gathering where someone remarked that he was just like them. He looked like them, had high-pressure jobs like them and would probably die early like them. Whether rational or not, whether he'd eaten a mountain of salad or not, the fear was just too strong. Especially since what the woman said made sense. There was no way Amber and he could keep up their "recreation" at the same levels. No one had that much endurance.

"Or," returned Amber calmly, "his pressure really is getting better. In which case, he needs less medication. Or he might pass out again when he stands up too quickly."

"I'm not so worried about him fainting as I am a stroke."

"But he doesn't have to do either! Just cut back on his meds."

Finally, the doctor turned to Amber. Her voice was almost kind, but Roger could feel the hauteur beneath the words. "I understand that you've been trying some New Age stuff to control his hypertension. But as a doctor, you know that genetics don't change, that a predisposition to high blood pressure guarantees that he will need medication for life. To suggest otherwise is wishful thinking at best. At worse, it's extremely dangerous."

Amber straightened, her voice colder than he had ever heard it before. "I didn't say take him off the medication, just cut it back. As for the rest..." She shook her head and sighed. "You have no idea what's possible and not possible, Dr. Hamilton."

In response, the doctor threw up her hands in what had to be a calculated display of temper. It conveyed the perfect blend of frustration with an idiot patient and overwhelming patience for remaining calm and rational with her next words.

"Mr. Martell, please consider what seems more logical to you. That prayer and New Age voodoo has miraculously reconstructed your DNA, or that your new diet and a ton of whoopee has *temporarily* helped your situation."

Roger bit his lip. Obviously, diet and sex made more scientific sense. But he really didn't want to say that. So he focused on the most logical compromise he could.

"Well, what if I stay on the diet and continue recreating whenever I want? Then my blood pressure will remain down and I can cut my medications. That sounds reasonable, doesn't it?"

Sadly, both women sighed and he had the oddest feeling that he had just said something wrong. Thankfully, Amber was able to explain it to him in a gentle voice.

"She doesn't believe you will stick to the diet, Roger. And frankly, given that you fainted at Dougie's Steak Barn, I can hardly blame her."

"I was going to the salad bar!" Roger huffed. Sadly, he'd forgotten to tell Sam to keep his mouth shut. And sure enough, the traitor had to speak up.

"But you ordered the halibut."

"Fish! Healthy, lean fish!"

Amber touched his hand. "It's okay. I never really expected you to stay on it completely. I just wanted to lower your pressure and build other foods back in slowly."

"Which is working," Roger said. How had everything turned around so that he was the bad guy? He lifted his chin. "I've made my decision," he said loudly. "I'm going to stop taking my pills."

He never thought to hear both women scream the same thing at the same time. In fact, he wondered if the nurse had spoken aloud, too, because suddenly his little cubicle echoed with one word: *"No!"*

He blinked. Okay. Clearly, not what he had expected. He turned to Amber, looking her in the eye. He didn't know the other doctor, and frankly, he didn't like her. Even if she did seem scientifically correct.

"What do you think I should do?"

But before Amber could speak, the doctor stepped forward, her voice calm and reasonable, and all the more powerful because what she said sounded so right.

"I'm the professional here, Mr. Martell. I'm the one with years of science and research on my side. I'm telling you to stay on the *full* dosage of your medication. If you continue to feel light-headed in six months—which is long enough to see if your recreation lasts—you and your regular doctor can discuss alternatives. Any other choice risks a cardiac event."

Roger opened his mouth to speak, but she would not let him get a word out. In fact, she flowed right into an impassioned speech that she must have given dozens of times.

"I see patients in here every day who try some New Age hocum only to have their entire lives destroyed by idiocy. Supplements, acupuncture, prayer trees, and the weirdest diets ever. They all think they know something that medical science hasn't found. Do not allow yourself to be victimized by that. Don't became another sad statistic. Please. You seem like a reasonable man. Go with reason now."

She stopped, and Roger had to admit that he was inclined to go with what she said. Science and medicine against meditation and a weird diet. Especially since she was right. As much as he might plan to stick to both—as well as the nightly sexfest—reality told him it wasn't going to happen. He'd started to tire of salad. Hell, he was completely fed up with green stuff. And the nightly sex couldn't possibly last.

He looked at Amber who read the answer in his eyes. She nodded and smiled gently at him.

"It's okay, Roger. You have to go with what seems right to you."

Roger released a slow breath of relief. Amber wasn't going to damn him for staying on his medication at the regular levels. But apparently she wasn't done yet. She turned to the doctor and spoke, her voice resigned, but no less compelling.

"Remember that day, Dr. Hamilton? The first day you realized you were just putting bandage after bandage on wounds that would never heal. Constant medication for conditions that shouldn't exist in a healthy person. Diabetics who had to turn their lives upside down to stay alive. Cures that might just be killing the patients slower instead of helping them."

"Science is never perfect," responded the woman, her voice

calmer now that she had won Roger over. "Medicine even less so. That doesn't mean it's wrong."

"One day—I hope one day soon—you'll get a larger perspective. And you'll wonder what huge piece of the puzzle you're missing. I didn't say medicine was wrong. I just think it doesn't know more than a tiny fraction of the whole."

"Of course, diet and prayer helps," Dr, Hamilton said with only a slight sneer. "But it'll never replace medication."

Amber wanted to argue. He could see it in every line of her body. But even he could tell that it would do no good. There didn't seem to be much common ground between the two women. Which was potentially very bad because that meant that Roger didn't have much in common with Amber either. After all, hadn't he just agreed with Hamilton about his medication?

"Never say never, Dr. Hamilton."

That was Amber's final word on the subject. Dr. Hamilton's as well, apparently, because the woman just shook her head and walked out. Roger thought Amber would make some excuse to leave, too. After all, she'd just lost a knock-down-drag-out with a bitch. But she didn't. She stayed by his side and held his hand. She didn't even make him feel like an ass for taking the other woman's advice over hers.

"Amber," he began, not even sure what he wanted to say.

She silenced him with a tender kiss to his lips. "Slow and steady is good, Roger. We'll keep an eye on your pressure. If it's down for good, we'll know, and you can start cutting back on your meds." Then she eyed him critically. "But until your fainting spells stop, I'm going to insist on driving you places."

He blinked. "Fainting *spells?* It was one time!"

"Or you could make an appointment with your regular doctor. Talk realistically about your new diet and that we are *not* going to cut back to once a week—"

He snorted. As if.

"Promise that I'll monitor your pressure daily, and see what he recommends."

Roger thought that over for about a half second. It took a little longer to frame his response.

"How much more than once a week?"

She smiled, but it was Sam in the corner who responded with a loud snort. "That's my cue to get some coffee. And call my fiancée. Maybe she'll be up for helping me moderate my pressure."

Roger didn't speak until Sam had disappeared around the curtain. Then he grabbed Amber by the shoulders and hauled her half on top of him. She squeaked in surprise, but relaxed against him almost immediately.

"How much?" he repeated. "How much more than once a week?"

"As much as you like," she said.

"Deal," he said, right before he kissed her.

AMBER WAITED OUTSIDE while the last of Roger's exit paperwork was done. She felt bruised inside and out and had needed to step away just to get enough space to breathe freely again.

Back in her loft, she was the authority on everything. People came to her, begging for her guidance. Whatever she said carried power and authority. But out here, back in the real world, she was butting heads against a larger foe than anything Spike could conjure. Out here, she was fighting the entire weight of the medical establishment. Sure they gave reluctant deference to the power of diet and meditation. Everyone agreed in the mind-body connection. But it was a fuzzy connection at best, and they put their real faith in pharmaceuticals.

She didn't. Which put her in a real disconnect with a large

portion of the medical establishment. Which left her exactly where?

Perversely enough, her argument with the oh-so-sure-of-herself Dr. Hamilton made her want to return to Mandolin more than ever. The E.R. doctor wasn't evil, just very set in her belief that chronic conditions could only be managed by drugs. Amber believed differently. What if hypertension was because a body's qi energy was out of whack? What if diabetes, arthritis, even attention deficit disorder could be corrected the same way?

She didn't know if it was true, but she sure as hell wanted someone asking the questions. *She* wanted to be asking the questions right here on the front lines in a high-profile hospital like Mandolin. And in a way that made the Dr. Hamiltons of the world *think* about their assumptions. Because that was the only way that medicine would evolve and grow into something better.

That's what she wanted. But was she delusional? Would she even be allowed to bring up the debate, much less address it in her own way? She didn't know. The directors she had talked to this evening had seemed open enough to the idea. But how many of them were on her side of the fence and how many on Dr. Hamilton's?

And what about Roger? His job, his life and his best friend was in Chicago. If she moved back to Arizona to fight the good fight, then what about him? What about their relationship?

They'd never last long distance. That never worked. So one of them would have to give up everything and move. She couldn't ask him to do that. Similarly, she wasn't sure she wanted to compromise her goals for him. There just weren't hospitals like Mandolin in Chicago. At least none that would look past why she'd been fired in the first place at what she brought to the table now.

She sighed and dropped her head back against the coarse

brick wall of the hospital. So, she supposed the real question went like this: Did she break up with Roger now? Or wait until their life choices and geography tore them apart?

19

AFTER THE DRAMA of the night before, the meeting the next day was anticlimactic. Sam and Jack got along great. Two nerds talking bioengineering. Roger didn't even need to be there, which was a good thing because he couldn't stop thinking about Amber.

He couldn't shake the feeling that something was wrong between them. After leaving the hospital, they had gone back to the hotel and collapsed into bed. He'd tried to talk to her, ask about her meeting with Jack, but she'd just yawned and shaken her head. This morning had been even worse. She'd been up and gone for breakfast with her parents while he and Sam had prepared for the meeting with Jack. In short, there was nothing he could do but wait it out and hope she talked to him.

So he went into business mode. He did what he could to charm Jack and not hate the man for his past relationship with Amber. He tried to listen closely enough to prevent the two geeks from planning something ridiculously expensive and completely impractical. And then he spent the rest of his time trying not to obsess about every word, every gesture that had gone on the night before. It didn't help that Amber was sitting in the conference room, too, looking cool and professional and so unlike the woman he'd gotten to know over the last two weeks.

In the end, he had to just man up and do his job. Amber was an adult. If she said everything between them was fine, then he would take her at her word. She'd tell him the truth when she was ready, and in the meantime, he had to focus on how Mandolin and RFE could work together. He managed. Barely. And he was never more thankful than when they stepped out of Mandolin and finally, blessedly, got onto the plane back to Chicago.

He hoped he'd get a chance to talk with Amber on the flight, but luck was not with him. Sam was practically high from the meeting, so bursting with ideas the man wouldn't shut up. While Amber buried her nose in a book, Roger ended up taking an entire pad of paper's worth of notes on what RFE's next big projects were going to be. Knowing Sam, there would be a ton more refinements by tomorrow morning, but at the moment, his friend needed someone to write like the wind and ask hard cost-benefit questions now. That was Roger's job and always had been. All girlfriend questions had to wait until later.

Except there was no later. They got to Chicago and went straight to bed. In separate homes. Roger didn't like it, but while they were in Arizona, Amber had received word from the police. Spike was in custody and no threat to anyone right then. Which meant that Roger had no legitimate reason to keep her with him that night. Especially since he was dropping with exhaustion as well.

The next day was work as usual, but Sam was in extra-productive mode. Everyone was scrambling to keep up, Roger more than everyone else because he also had to make up for the two weeks of vacation he'd just taken. So he set his sights on the weekend, praying that Amber wouldn't choose to break up with him by email while he was buried deep in accounting projections.

Except, of course, that he forgot one thing: Sam's wedding. The man was getting married that weekend. There were all the usual festivities, of course, and a very full schedule of events for both groom and best man.

Thankfully, Sam was the very opposite of an anxious bridegroom. He and Julie were so very much in love that Sam was bursting with joy. "Bursting" being the key word because when Sam got happy, he got productive engineering-wise. If the man got any happier, RFE would have to triple in staff just to cover the extra work.

Which left even less time for Roger to spend with Amber. He did manage to see his doctor, though. He'd had two near fainting moments and was more convinced than ever that his dosage was too high. Surprisingly, his doctor was fascinated with what he and Amber had been doing. He had a ton of questions Roger wasn't even remotely qualified to answer. After twenty minutes of grilling, the man wrote the lower dose prescription almost as an afterthought. Truthfully, Roger didn't care what the man thought. He was going to go with a lower dosage just so Amber would be forced to take his blood pressure daily as she'd promised.

She did, of course. With every appearance of love and concern for him. But something was wrong between them. He was sure of it. She was preoccupied and remote, but every time he thought they could get a moment to talk, he was called back to work. Sam had another brilliant breakthrough. Or the lab caught on fire—again.

In short, he was as preoccupied and distracted as she was. They had to have it out. He couldn't live like this—questioning everything, watching for a sign or a clue. They had to talk. But when? And how? Between his schedule and her saying everything was fine, he couldn't find an opening.

The night before the wedding, he reached his wit's end. He needed help big time, so he grabbed his best friend and abducted him. But they didn't go the usual prewedding stripper bar—Sam couldn't care less about that kind of stuff. Instead, they went to the lab and together they began to plot.

AMBER GOT THE CALL three days after their return to Chicago. It was from the director of Mandolin, the same man who had fired her two years earlier. He'd been hearing great things about her, he said, from the board members she'd talked to at dinner, from Jack and from her parents. Yes, he and her father still golfed every Wednesday and Saturday mornings.

He asked her about what she'd been doing in the last two years. She answered with the right amount of spin, explaining her research and her conclusions, and framing it all in terms that would be the most palatable to him. He countered by saying that, yes, her old boss was retiring and it was only now that the director was seeing how very damaging that man had been to Mandolin. In short, he should have taken more time to think about her resignation two years earlier. She responded with appropriate contrition. She'd been young and impulsive. She understood the value of procedure and policy now that she was so much older and wiser.

And then came the final clinch. He said that the world was a new place, that patients were insisting on using the internet to help with their diagnoses and treatments, and that Mandolin could really use a doctor who spoke "New Age bullshit, no offense." She'd laughed and lied that she hadn't been insulted at all. That had resulted in an invitation to meet next week in Arizona to discuss her career.

It wasn't a job offer, but with the right maneuvering, it would be. She could probably step back into her old job as if she'd never left.

She was still staring at her phone, wondering what to do

and wishing Roger had time to talk when something completely unexpected happened. Roger's doctor called.

AMBER LOVED A WEDDING. Ever since she'd been the flower girl for her aunt when she was five, she'd had an addiction to white lace and rose petals. She'd secretly watched every reality TV show about wedding dresses, speciality cakes, and best of all, bridezillas. But actually attending weddings? That hadn't happened so much.

She'd always been too busy and too focused to develop the friendships that got someone invited to big events. She'd been to the odd relative's wedding, but even that had felt obligatory. Today, however, was all about fun.

She really liked Sam, and from what he'd said, she thought she and Julie could be friends. Plus, it was obvious that the man was head over heels in love. She'd known it from the tone of his voice and the way his eyes got dreamy when he spoke of her. When geeks fell in love, they fell hard and Sam was no exception. Roger had let slip that their courtship had gone beyond the usual series of dates. He hadn't said more, but she was intrigued.

She dressed with care, wearing a simple dress and sweater combo with low heels. She was sick to death of her stiletto boots. It wasn't her anymore, and she was planning on giving them to Goodwill. She was also sick to death of angsting over her relationship with Roger.

It was a simple question. Did she pursue the job at Mandolin or risk everything on her relationship with Roger? Her head said to go the practical route and the job in Arizona, but her heart said Roger was The One. But how could she possibly know that? They hadn't even known each other a month. They still had some major philosophical differences. He was science all the way, and she often thought she was getting weirder by the day. But on the other hand, stranger couples had worked.

And maybe he could come to accept something other than traditional medicine. Maybe...

So she dressed and went to the wedding, willing herself to stop thinking about her relationship with Roger. Except when she walked into the huge church, there he was, dressed in a tuxedo that made her knees melt. Sweet heaven, he was gorgeous. And when he spotted her in the door, his face lit with a joy akin to what Sam had when he spoke of Julie. Lord, she wanted to believe he loved her that much. She wished it could be true for her. But inside she worried she was just deluding herself. They were just too different.

Still, she couldn't stop staring at him. What would she give to be with him forever? To wake up every morning with him beside her? To walk down the aisle and have him standing there at the altar waiting for her?

"You look like you're about to cry," he whispered when he came to her side. "Are you all right?"

"I have a terrible confession to make," she whispered back. "I'm one of those horribly weepy women at weddings."

He smiled, but the worry didn't leave his expression. And that's when she started looking at him as a doctor. There were lines of fatigue around his eyes, and she felt a tension in his shoulders.

"What about you?" she asked as he started escorting her down the aisle to her seat. "You're looking tired."

"It's been a busy week," he said, his voice terribly... neutral.

She looked at him. She knew he'd been busy with work. And as Homeless Tammy had come down with a nasty cough and was now sleeping it off on her couch, Amber hadn't really had the space in her schedule for him. She'd managed to see him every day, checking his blood pressure and the like, but beyond that, they'd had no time together.

"Look, I've got responsibilities here," he said into her ear as he sat her down toward the front. "But I've got something important to show you."

"Roger, perhaps it would be best if—"

"Can't talk right now," he said, glancing hurriedly down the aisle. She followed his gaze, wondering what was making him so anxious. There were more than enough handsome ushers—the bride's brothers, she believed—to carry the load. But he didn't give her a chance to ask. "Promise you'll come with me tonight after the reception."

She sighed. "Roger, you're going to be exhausted. You should rest."

He arched a brow. "Exhausted? Hardly. Plastered is more likely, in which case, you'll have to drive me home."

She frowned. She highly doubted that he would get drunk. He just wasn't the type to binge drink, even at his best friend's wedding. "We'll get a cab—" she began, but again he cut her off.

"Promise me, Amber. Please."

She bit her lip and nodded. "Of course. Whatever you need."

THE WEDDING LIVED UP to Amber's expectations. Julie was even more stunning than she'd expected and Sam couldn't stop grinning. And Amber started grinning right along with them, especially when an octopus-like robot with a white veil acted as flower girl. It rolled up the aisle, trailing rose petals beneath its wheels, and even had a little fan that made the veil billow out behind it.

It was the most adorable thing Amber had ever seen. But she had no idea why one of the octopus arms carried a small strap that would normally attach to a weight machine. Still, the ideas that popped into her mind were interesting. And one glance at Roger told her he was thinking the same thing as he flashed her a grin.

She supposed her favorite moment of the ceremony was when the bride and groom exchanged vows. Both of them spoke so clearly and with such conviction that goose bumps prickled up and down Amber's arms. They were so sure. One look at them, and there was no question in their eyes or their hearts. They could vow forever because they were that in love.

Tears slid down Amber's face and she discreetly wiped them away. What was this? She was a career woman all the way. Dedicated to her research, to changing the face of Western medicine. She was not someone who got weepy over a guy. And yet, obviously, she was. She wanted to be with Roger forever.

She sighed and refocused on the bride and groom. They were lighting a unity candle, the warm glow of the flame perfectly illuminating their smiles. A moment later, they were pronounced husband and wife, and Sam kissed his bride.

And what a kiss it was! He touched Julie's face with such reverence and then slowly pressed his lips to hers. It was so tender that Amber teared up again. And then the little robot released a horn fanfare and blew out confetti over everyone. Cheers erupted, applause and more robotic whistles. Sam and Julie were married.

And Amber needed another pack of tissue.

HOURS LATER, Amber's eyes had dried. She had gorged herself on the huge buffet. Beer and brats were the theme—apparently the groom's choice—but there was ample food for her. And the best chocolate wedding cake she'd ever tasted. Interestingly enough, the cake had been done up as an elevator with the bride and groom inside. It was quite the picture, and Amber had been blessed with getting the Door Close button. As she had her own fond memories of the RFE elevator, she took it as a special gift.

But now the food was nearly gone, her head was fuzzy from the champagne and she'd lost track of the number of handsome groomsmen who had asked her to dance. And there were quite a number of handsome groomsmen. Sadly, the only one she cared about had been conspicuously absent. Amber was just thinking it was time to leave despite her promise to Roger when the man in question grabbed the microphone.

"Excuse me, excuse me. If I could have everyone's attention please?"

Roger's voice was commanding, but in that tux he didn't need to say a word to grab every woman's attention. Females from the age of three to a hundred and three had been on him all night long. Yes, Amber realized as she drained the last of her champagne, she had been counting. He'd danced or spoken to no less than fifty-seven of the opposite sex during the reception, and not a one of them had been her. And now he was launching into a speech.

"Love is a weird thing," he said into the microphone. "Six months ago, I would have said that Sam could only love a woman made of metal. Obviously, I was wrong." And right on cue, the little robot let out a mournful whistle.

Everyone laughed, and Roger waited the appropriate amount of time before continuing. "Here's the thing. No robot, no matter how good, no science, no electronics could come close to creating the changes I've seen in my best friend since Julie stepped into his life. First off, the man has finally left his lab. No kidding. I ask you all, look at his face. Sam has a tan. When did you ever think that would happen? Probably about the same time I stopped eating cooked food. In short, never—but love has a way of doing that to a man."

Amber frowned, her gaze sharpening on Roger's face. He wasn't looking at her at the moment, but his words suggested he was talking to her. But that couldn't be. Damn. She pushed away her glass. She shouldn't have been drinking so much. It made her think things that couldn't be true.

"Second," Roger continued, "Sam's more creative than he's ever been, and that's saying something. Since he met Julie, he's worked better, thought better and done more than ever before, and believe me when I say he was no slouch before."

Roger lowered his voice a bit, his gaze turning directly to Amber. "That's something, isn't it? Change for the better. That's real love and real risk because it's hard to change. But obviously, his lady love is worth it."

He paused then—a long kind of awkward pause—as his gaze continued to hold hers. Amber shifted nervously as others began to notice. Everyone was looking at her, wondering who she was and what Roger was really saying. Everyone including her.

And then the moment was over. Roger turned back to the happy couple. "Thank you, Julie, for changing my friend into something better. May we all find exactly what you have."

Applause erupted all around. Glasses were raised and good wishes abounded. But Roger didn't stick around for them. One moment he was up at the front of the stage, giving Julie a kiss and shaking Sam's hand. Then a second later, the microphone was resting on the table, and he was nowhere to be found.

Amber frowned. Where had he gone? What—

Her mind stuttered to a halt as a familiar hand crept around her waist.

"It's time," Roger whispered into her ear.

"What?" she gasped.

"It's time for a change," he said. Then he took her arm and half escorted, half carried her out the door.

20

"WHERE ARE WE GOING?" she asked, as she sank into his car's soft bucket seats. She ought to object. He was being awfully high-handed with her. But it had been a lovely wedding, a lovely night and she'd had a lot of lovely champagne. Besides, she was tired of her own thinking, so she resolved to stop. Let him lead her. He always had good ideas anyway.

Or so she thought until he did *not* head toward his apartment. Or her loft. She straightened, peering into the streets. "Roger?"

"I need to talk to you."

She snorted. "Roger, tonight is probably not the best night for talking. I'm more than a little buzzed."

"Perfect," he said, then he swung into the RFE building's underground parking.

Amber closed her eyes. Obviously, Roger had something planned, but she had to stop him now before he went any further.

"They want me back at Mandolin," she blurted out. Then she opened her eyes and turned to look at Roger. He had stilled, his entire body quieting, so she filled the silence with her jumbled thoughts. "The director called yesterday. He wants me to fly out on Monday to talk about how I could fit back into my old job."

"Are you going?" he asked, his voice unnaturally quiet.

She nodded. "Nothing's for sure. It's just to talk about possibilities."

"But it's a prelude to an offer, right?"

She nodded, feeling miserable.

"And it's what you want." It wasn't a question, but she took it as one anyway.

"It's where I've been headed since before I met you. In fact, meeting you was the first step to getting back there. But…" She closed her eyes again, knowing she was handling this badly. This wasn't a topic to discuss when she was buzzed, much less right after the most romantic wedding she'd ever seen. It made her wish for all the things she'd long ago given up to pursue medicine.

Then she felt his hand, gentle as he pulled her chin back toward him. "But…?" he prompted.

She sighed. "But you don't live in Arizona."

His smile was slow in coming but no less beautiful. "So you haven't decided on the job there."

"No."

"So there's still time to talk you out of it."

She sighed. Was there? "We're so different, and we've only known each other a few weeks. We're both driven by our careers. And—"

He silenced her with a kiss. It was a gentle one, but highly insistent and very distracting. And when it was done, her arms were wound around his neck and her body was as plastered against him as she could get in a car.

"Stop thinking," he said, in a perfect echo of the words she'd said to him so many times.

She sighed. "I've been trying, but my brain won't shut up."

He smiled. "Then trust me for a little bit longer, okay? Besides, it involves a trip up in the elevator."

She laughed. "Okay, fine. But you're the only guy I know who can tempt me with a ride in a freight elevator."

He grinned, then helped her step out of his car. Her heels were low, her dress modest compared to what she used to wear a couple years back. But the light in his eyes when he looked at her legs made her feel like she was still outfitted in the latest designer do-me suit. And just to prove it, she added a little wiggle to her hips.

He growled behind her. "Okay, that's going to completely derail tonight's plan."

She looked over her shoulder. "And that's a bad thing?"

He sobered, and she caught desperation in his expression. "Yeah," he said softly. "It would be. So we're going to keep this particular elevator ride platonic."

"Spoilsport," she huffed as the elevator doors opened. She stepped inside, wondering if she could change his mind. So she leaned back against the wall and stretched her legs out in front of her. A come-hither look in her eyes and a pretend itch, right above her hemline, had her lifting the edge of her skirt.

The doors closed, the motor kicked into gear, and Roger settled across the elevator from her. He was certainly watching her, his eyes smoldering, but he didn't move so much as a finger.

"Hmmm," she murmured. "You are being rather focused right now. What are you up to?"

He didn't move except to lift his gaze from her exposed thigh to her eyes. And then he spoke. "Sex has never been our problem."

Amber froze, abruptly wishing that she hadn't enjoyed the excellent bar at the reception. She wasn't ready to face whatever Roger had in mind. Not if it wasn't about sex and only sex. Not if—

"Stop thinking so much, Amber." He blinked, his expression shifting into surprise. "Wow, I never thought I'd be saying that to you, much less have to say it twice."

"I'm the original stuck-in-her-head girl. Why do you think I gravitated to energy healing? It forced me to quiet my brain."

He smiled, his expression softening in the way that made her belly liquefy and her heart pitter-patter. "Just let me lead for the moment, okay? I swear it'll be okay."

She nodded. What else could she do? She didn't feel capable of taking charge anymore. Not now. Not in her life, even. And certainly not in their relationship. So she waited in silence as the elevator ground to a halt.

Moments later, they were walking through RFE and into Roger's office. She'd been in here once before, back on that first day when she'd been determined to get his attention. She'd been dressed to dominate then, and she'd known just what to do. Now she was in a dress and sweater and low heels. Not exactly power attire. And yet, when Roger gestured her to the seat across from his gleaming, *empty* desk top, she realized he was nervous. His hands were shaking the tiniest bit, and he kept stroking the folds of his cummerbund as if to smooth it.

She settled down in the chair, her mind stuttering with confusion while he brought his computer to life with a few keystrokes.

"Roger…"

"It'll be easier if you sit here at my desk," he said.

She nodded, rising slowly to come around and settle into his executive chair. Lord, it had molded to his body, the scent of leather and him rising up to fill her senses as she dropped into the chair. He wasn't even touching her but standing to the side, and yet she felt completely enfolded by him.

"Okay," he said, "here's the thing. We're going to play a game. There are right answers and wrong answers to a series of questions. If you get it right, then I forfeit an item of clothing. If you get it wrong, then it's you who will be getting naked."

She grinned. "Strip questions. Sounds great to me, but why don't we go to your home—"

He shook his head. "First question. Are you thinking about breaking up with me?"

She swallowed, her buzz abruptly gone. But maybe it was better this way. Rip the bandage off quick. But she couldn't bring herself to say it. Instead, she looked at him. "Have you ever had a long-distance relationship that worked?"

He shook his head. "No. You?"

"No."

He sighed, then spun his cummerbund around and unhooked it.

She blinked in surprise. "That was the right answer?"

"It was an honest answer, which is all I want from you. And I think it's pretty clear that I'm the loser in that statement, so this comes off." He pulled the thick fabric away and set it aside.

"You do know that you have like ten times more clothes on than I do, right?"

He gave her a rueful smile. "I expect that you'll be getting most of the answers right. After all, all you have to do is answer honestly."

She stood up from his desk, her mood gone. She'd done the hard part. She'd told him about the job in Arizona and what it meant to her. The rest was too painful to delve into right now. "I don't like this game, Roger. In fact, I don't like games at all. Not about something this important."

He moved to block her escape. "That's a lie, Amber. You do like games. You just don't like games where you're not in control."

"That's bull—"

"How we met was a game—is Roger gay or not? My whole diet change was a game, too—living foods or die."

"I didn't phrase it like that!"

He grimaced. "Yes, you kinda did. The point was, if I wanted to play your game—and I definitely did—then I had to play by your rules. Living foods."

"Your blood pressure is better."

"Yes, it is. And you owe me a piece of clothing because you *do* like games."

He folded his arms across his chest, looking very impressive as his tux jacket perfectly defined the dimensions of his torso. Of course he was using his dominant appearance to keep her playing. So she sighed and thought about the truth. Yes, she liked playing games—sudoku, poker, was the hot executive gay, could she find the right diagnosis in time—all of those were games of one sort or another. So she huffed, giving in with little grace.

"Fine. You're right. I do like games." She shrugged out of her sweater. Which left her precious few pieces of clothing left. After all, she was in a dress.

"Good. Now comes the harder part, but here we go. You believe we don't have a future together."

She arched a brow. "Too easy. I mean, isn't that the reason everyone breaks up?"

He nodded. "True enough. All right. How's this? You think that because I went with Dr. Hamilton's prescription in Arizona that at heart I'm a science guy while you, on the other hand, have been out on the woo-woo edge for a long time. That puts us, in your mind, at opposite ends of the spectrum.

Am I right? So why bother sticking around if our relationship isn't going to work anyway?"

She felt her eyes widen in shock. He had described exactly what she'd been dithering over for the last few days. Which meant that he felt it, too. He *knew* it, too. Her vision suddenly went blurry with tears and she had to look away rather than lose it in front of him.

"Amber," he said gently, pulling her face back to his. "Just answer. Is that what you think?"

She didn't speak, but the tears that dripped from her lashes must have been answer enough. He wiped them away with his thumb, and she couldn't stop herself from nuzzling into his touch. Then he dropped a soft kiss onto her lips before pulling back. "It'll be all right, Amber. Just stay with me a bit longer, okay?"

She didn't honestly see how anything could be okay ever again, but she nodded because he wanted her to. Then he straightened and pulled off his jacket. He took a deep breath and looked her in the eye.

"You're wrong, Amber. Dead wrong."

"No, I'm not. You work in robotics, every argument we've ever had included you saying things like energy voodoo and yin-yang yipperdo. I believe in this stuff, Roger. So don't tell me that I'm wrong. We don't agree on this and I don't think we ever will."

He nodded grimly as he reached up and pulled off his tie. His motions were sharp, almost angry, but there was no lessening of determination in his tightened jaw.

"Next phase," he said, her voice rigidly controlled. "Self-examination. You think you know me, and you may be right, but I submit that you don't know *you* well enough to see the real problem."

"Bullshit."

He gestured to the computer. "Next comes a series of

scientific and lateral-thinking puzzles. You're going to answer them one by one, then the computer will tell you if you were able to answer them correctly faster than I did yesterday."

"I'm half drunk," she lied. In truth, her buzz was completely gone.

"All the better," he said. "I have a chance."

No, he really didn't. Academic tests, lateral thinking, she had started taking these things while she was still in diapers. And she couldn't even blame it on her parents. She loved these damn games.

She shot one more look at her boyfriend-for-a-few-more-minutes. His face was resolved, his eyes desperate. She didn't know what he was trying to accomplish here, but obviously he wanted a resolution. Very well. She did, too. But if she was about to break up with the only man she ever loved, then he was damn well going to be naked when he did it.

With sudden resolve, she turned her attention to his computer and getting Roger out of his clothes.

21

OKAY, SO EVEN DRUNK, Amber was brilliant, and he was down to trousers and one sock. It's not that his answers were bad. Hell, he'd gotten them *right*. But she had gotten them right faster. All except for one question and that's because she'd wasted time arguing with the computer's answer. The software itself was flawed, she'd claimed.

And to make matters worse, what was the one item she'd taken off? Her thong. Yes, her thong. She'd stood up, reached under her dress, and slid it down her legs. He didn't get to see anything good. Didn't even get to touch the lacy thing, as she tossed it to the opposite side of the room. Then she sat back down and crossed her beautiful legs, driving him nuts with the idea that she was completely naked beneath that dress. Hell, she wasn't even wearing stockings. Meanwhile, he was half naked and harder than a rock.

"So, what have we proved here?" she asked.

He leaned forward. "That you still think like a scientist. That mentally you still hang out in the realm that Sam and his geeks do. You even describe your energy healing as research, not fact. Ergo, you're more *scientific* than I am."

She squirmed as he pinned her with his gaze. "Ergo?" she mocked.

"I passed the test, too, Amber. I live and work with you people every day. Some of the lingo wears off."

She blinked at him, and he saw reluctant agreement come over her features. "Fine. You win that one." She obligingly kicked off her shoes. "I'm a geek. What about it?"

"So that pulls you back from the far end of the weirdness scale. You're not swallowing the latest fad whole hog. You think about it. You study it. In fact, I'd bet that you're proud of that. You look for the reasons behind, the physics and the spiritual combined."

She'd dropped her chin into her palm, and stared at him unblinkingly from that position. He thought for a moment that she might have zoned out, but he was wrong. A second later, she straightened and pulled off her necklace. "Good bet. You're right."

He exhaled in relief. "Now for phase three. Thank God, because this is the part where you get naked."

"Oh, really?" she drawled.

"Really," he shot back. "This is where I prove that I've been living in the woo-woo world much longer than you have."

"Ha!" she shot back, and he grinned.

"True or false—I've been doing astrology almost since before I was born."

She didn't even think twice. "False."

"True." Then as proof, he pulled open his bottom drawer. He had to unlock it first which just went to show how embarrassed he was about this whole thing, but humiliation was a necessary evil tonight. And there was too much on the line to avoid revealing this to her.

As she watched in shock, he pulled out his astrological chart, then another one for his perfect mate, and then there was hers—or as much of it as he could do given that he didn't know the exact time she had been born.

She frowned as she carefully paged through the charts.

He didn't miss that she understood what she was looking at. Astrology must have been one of the things she'd studied.

"You did my chart yesterday," she said softly, lifting up her sheet.

"Yeah." He leaned over her, and her hair brushed across his naked skin. It was all he could do not to extend that caress across his chest and to slip his hands around her in the process.

"Impressive," she said softly. "How did you learn this?"

"My mother was deeply into astrology but Dad kept having a fit at how much she was spending on it. So he offered me a deal. He paid me to learn everything I could about it and figure out how to chart Mom. I needed the money, so I agreed." He noticed that his hand had trailed across her shoulder and had to force himself to step backward. "It's really rather scientific once you get into it. A whole system of numbers and computations."

She nodded. "I know." Then she pierced him with her dark gaze. "And how accurate has it been for you?"

He shrugged. "Anywhere from twelve to seventy percent depending on how accurately you label the predictions. You know, 'significant breakthrough in career' might mean that Sam gets a new idea for a product. Or it might mean that we'll get a new contract. Or it could just mean that I'll have one day where nothing goes wrong. That would be a miracle in and of itself."

She tilted her head. "So you don't really believe."

"Do you?"

She hedged as she flipped to the chart of his ideal mate. He'd highlighted the areas where she and his ideal lined up, and her fingers danced over one bright yellow streak after another. "I believe that belief creates more belief. And that even with a chart that points to the exact opposite direction, people will see what they need to see in it."

He lifted his chin. "So we're agreed. *Exactly* agreed on astrology. I believe you owe me a dress."

She laughed as she pulled a diamond stud out of her ear. "You get an earring."

He sighed. Just as well. He was having a hard enough time keeping his hands off her as it was. Take her out of that dress, and he wouldn't see this game through to the end.

"Next question," he growled at her. Predictably, she just smiled and he lost himself for a moment in her beauty. And damn her, she took advantage of his distraction.

"This has been lots of fun, but we're not really making progress here."

And right there he got angry. He'd held it together so far because he'd spent hours on this particular game and was determined to see it through. And also because he was slowly and surely getting her naked. That always brightened his mood. But she wasn't *listening* and she sure as hell wasn't *seeing* what he wanted her to. And so he let his temper out to play.

She'd been turning his desk chair to stand up, but he didn't let her. Instead, he dropped his hands on the armrests, blocked her into the seat, and lowered his face to hers.

"Next question," he said. "Do you know why I'm a leader? How I make more money than Sam in his own company? How not-so-brilliant me can lead an entire herd of genius cats?"

She swallowed, obviously startled by his suddenly aggressive stance. But she wasn't one to back down, so she simply looked him in the eye. "Because you're not as stupid as you pretend."

He snorted as he jerked his chin back at the computer. "Do I have to show you my scores again? Compare them to yours? Or Sam's, by the way? Or just about anyone else in this company? Believe me when I say that *everyone* at RFE knows that they're smarter than I am. And yet I still lead them. And even Sam knows I'm the best man for the job. Why?"

He could see her struggling with that answer because in her world, the smartest ought to be the best leaders. And, of course, she and every other academic in the world was dead wrong.

"Because I see strengths where they just see data sets. I feel when someone's about to break under the strain and when someone needs to be pushed. I study the market and the world, and figure out what works and what doesn't."

She nodded. "Of course. You're marketing—"

"I'm intuitive, Amber. You honestly think I understand half of what passes for conversation around here? Dream on! I don't read their memos, I read *them*. I don't look at the client specs, I look at their lives and their needs. I *intuit* what has to happen next, and if you don't think that's out on the woo-woo edge, then you haven't sat one day in my office and seen anything I do."

She blinked, obviously stunned by what he'd revealed. "You don't read their memos?"

"Have you ever tried to read a geek memo? It's either so technical I need a translator or it's all rambling thoughts—"

"—that can't possibly make sense to someone else."

He nodded at the understanding that had come into her voice. At the shift from shock to awe with an underlayer of delight. "You understand," he whispered, thrilled beyond measure. So he kissed her. He pressed his lips to hers and just feasted as he'd wanted to all night long.

She arched into his touch, opened for his plunder, and even wrapped an arm around his neck to draw him closer. He did what she wanted—what they both wanted—for a moment. And then he pulled himself back, pressing his forehead to hers as he caught his breath.

"We're a lot closer than you think," he whispered.

"You're right," she said. She stood, pushing his office chair away as she did. Then she reached behind her back and pulled down the zipper of her dress. It fell apart slowly, the sound going straight to his groin. And shock of all shocks, she was braless beneath the dress. It had a tight bodice inside it, and now she peeled it away.

One second, she was demurely clothed except for her bare feet. The next second, she stood before him in nothing at all. Oh, God, he was going to explode. Then she stroked her hand down his chest, her fingertips trailing fire across his skin.

"Come closer," she urged.

He groaned. His stomach was still rippling with her touch, and his dick did its best to push its way through his pants. Any other day, he would have succumbed right then and there. She was hot and he was hard. And better yet, he'd just forced a huge concession from her. She'd admitted that their world-views weren't quite as far apart as she'd thought.

But Sam had just married his true love. Roger had seen the joy and the terror that had gripped his best friend during the entire courtship. And it had taken a great deal from Julie to get his friend to see what they both wanted.

It was no different with Amber. And this time, it had to be him—the leader—to help her take the last step. And he couldn't allow himself to sink into her sweet body until she had.

"Amber," he said as he began kissing down the side of her face. "I love you. And I intend to marry you."

He felt his words hit her like little bombs. Her body abruptly went tight, her breath stuttered in tiny gasps, and her hands slowly pulled backward off his body.

Oh, hell. She was pulling away. Time for phase four.

22

AMBER STRUGGLED WITH PANIC. He had *not* just said those words. He had *not* just said *marry*. Except he had. And she was all but hyperventilating at the thought.

"Don't panic," he said softly.

"I don't panic," she returned tartly. But of course she did panic. She *was* panicking. Things were progressing way too fast. Fifteen minutes ago, she'd told him she was going out to Arizona for a job at Mandolin. Now he was talking marriage? She bit her lip, wondering how quickly she could get her dress back on. She needed to think and standing here naked was not the way to do it.

Snick.

She looked down at her wrist in shock. She had to blink twice before her brain could process what she saw. Had Roger just handcuffed her to his desk? No way.

Yes, way. How had she not seen when he'd pulled open one of his desk drawers? How had she not noticed when he'd reached in and retrieved a cuff? Now it was around her wrist and the other end was attached to—she jerked her hand upright—an incredibly solid bar. On the inside of his desk drawer.

"What the hell is this for?" she demanded. "And why do you have it in there?"

"It's to keep you from running. And I installed it yesterday for just this event."

She gaped at him. "What?"

"Phase four," he said. "Hold on. There's something on the other side." He pulled open the other drawer. She should have seen it coming. I mean, how stupid was she to fall for the same trick twice? But she leaned over to see what he was pulling out of his other desk drawer, only to see that it was another handcuff as it snapped on her other wrist.

She was now held arms apart facing him, with her butt braced against his desk top. And she was naked.

"Not the typical marriage proposal," she drawled, but with an edge of anger to her voice.

"This isn't a proposal," he said. "I said I *intend* to marry you."

One look in his eyes told her that he was serious. Perversely, that eased some of the fear in her chest. But if he wasn't asking her to marry him, what was he doing?

"Most ministers balk at the sight of a handcuffed bride."

His lips twitched, but he didn't smile. "As I said, this is phase four. The lie detector test."

She glanced around the room. Nowhere did she see electrodes or a machine to read biosignals. All she saw was Roger, looking almost grim as he ran his hands lightly down her body.

She shivered at his caress, trying to tell herself it was from cold or fear or any one of those emotions. But it wasn't. Whatever "phase four" was, it wasn't going to hurt her. On some level, it was kinda fun.

So she leaned forward as far as she could reach, and began licking tiny nips across his chest. "Kinky," she murmured. "But apparently, I'm into it."

His belly tightened and she could hear the hammer of his heart. If she didn't know for a fact that his blood pressure was down, she might even be worried. As it was, she smiled when she heard his groan rumble through him.

"Amber," he growled. "You're distracting me."

"It's only fair. You handcuffed me."

He reached forward, cupped her face in his hands, and drew it up to his. His fingers were gentle as he stroked her cheeks, and his eyes were dark with hunger. "You realize what you just said doesn't make sense."

She shrugged. "Bondage doesn't make logical sense."

He pressed a long, slow kiss to her mouth. He started simply, nipping along her lips, but she quickly grew tired of that. Let him find out that there were a ton of things that she could do without the use of her hands.

So she abruptly invaded his mouth, and a moment later, they were fused together, dueling as only two alpha mates can. His hands slid up her hips to cup her breasts. Now she was the one growling as his fingers found and pinched her nipples.

Her thighs widened and he stepped between the V created. Her legs wrapped around his, drawing him closer against her. She wanted to rub her body along his. She wanted him inside her. She wanted to do all of that right now because otherwise she might have to think about what he had said not more than a minute ago.

Then he pulled away. He didn't step backward; her legs were too tight for him to move far. But he broke their kiss and his hands stilled on her breasts.

"I think you're afraid of commitment," he said.

"Wrong." She made a loud buzzer noise. "Now take off your pants."

He shook his head. "Let's look at the facts, shall we? We'll start with your move to Chicago. You got put in a terrible position—caught between your desire to heal and the politics of the hospital. So instead of fighting, you up and move to Chicago."

She blinked. "I got fired, Roger. That's not—"

"It wasn't leaving Arizona that's the issue, Amber. It's that you didn't go work in another hospital, that you didn't open your own practice how you wanted it. You disappeared into Cherry Hills."

She tilted her head back, trying to fight the tears. After all this time, didn't he understand? "I don't know that I could have been hired anywhere else—"

"Bullshit."

She jumped a little bit at his harsh tone. Then she was forced to nod. "Okay, maybe I could have. But I needed time for the research. I didn't just magically understand astrology. I had to learn about it. Same with all the other modalities." Then she straightened as much as she could. "And here's the really important part, Roger. I'm going back. I'm stepping back into the fight."

"Are you? Or are you just running from me? From us?"

She blinked, wondering at his words. Then she forced herself to look him in the eye. "I'm not running," she whispered. "I'm torn up about it. I want to stay, Roger. But I want to go back to Mandolin, too."

He touched her face, a slow caress that ended with his thumb on her lower lip, slowly stroking back and forth. Her mouth swelled under his touch and her mind fuzzed out. "Progress," he whispered. Then he abruptly straightened. "Next piece of evidence—the way we met. You approached me under a false identity, seduced me in the elevator and told me it was all because of a bet."

"It was! And because you're kinda sexy hot," she added, wiggling her hips enough to make him gasp.

"Right," he said, his hands going to her hips to hold her still.

"That's not fear, Roger. That's lust, pure and simple."

He nodded, and she was pleased to see that he was having trouble keeping focused. Good thing because she was, too. "Actually, it was you making it clear that we were just a one-time thing. A bet. A hot elevator hookup. Not a relationship."

"Well, I got that wrong, didn't I?"

"Yeah, you did. Because I pursued you. I got you to help me. I went on your diet, and I basically forced myself into your life."

She frowned. He had forced himself in, hadn't he? And she had fought him all the way, to no avail. "But I wasn't panicking," she said, as much to him as to herself. "We had a great couple weeks."

"Yeah, because you knew that you had an escape—your old job in Arizona."

"That was the point of connecting with you. As an excuse to get back to Mandolin to check things out." She huffed. "Roger, this is ridiculous. I am not afraid of commitment!"

"Really? Then why is it that the moment we start getting serious, we suddenly have irreconcilable differences?"

She shook her head. "That's not how it happened."

"Wasn't it? I've been calling your work energy voodoo from the very beginning. But only after Arizona did it become a big problem."

She would have slammed her hands on his chest, would have shoved him away and walked out on his silly theories, but he had cuffed her to his desk. Cuffed. And so she could only shove him back from her with her head. He moved, but only an inch and her traitorous legs missed his heat and pressure immediately.

"This conversation is over," she snapped. "If this is what

you call your intuition, then I'm here to tell you that your radar is definitely off."

"Really?" he said, his voice dropping to a sultry challenge. "Care to put the theory to the test?"

She blinked. She hadn't expected him to get all calm and cat-ate-the-canary happy at what she'd just said. It took her a moment to put the pieces together, but then she did. Phase four was a lie detector test.

"You want to prove that I'm lying with some sort of detector."

He nodded. "Yup."

She huffed. "There's all sorts of problems with that idea, you know. The reliability is shaky, you don't have the equipment, and besides, it would test beliefs, not truth. If I believe what I'm saying, the test will read true."

He folded his arms. "And I'm saying that your body knows the truth even if your mind doesn't. You game?"

"You're being ridiculous. Just because I'm nervous about getting serious with you doesn't mean that I'm afraid of commitment."

He snorted. "I have news for you, Amber. We are serious. *I've* never been more serious in my life. So I ask you again, are you willing to put it to the test? Do you want to know if you really are afraid of commitment?" He leaned forward until they were nearly eye to eye. "Of becoming committed to *me?*"

She swallowed. It was a trick. Another tease in an entire evening of games. But if there was one thing she was good at, it was games. So she lifted her chin in defiance. "Bring it on. But when we're done, you're going to uncuff me. And then you're going to do exactly what I tell you." He arched his eyebrows, but she didn't let him ask the question. She just barreled on. "*Exactly* what I tell you, even if it's to drive me home and never contact me again."

He blanched at that, but she wasn't going to let him off the hook. After all, she was the one sitting spread-eagle, naked and cuffed to his desk. He needed to risk something, too.

"Deal," he said.

"Deal," she echoed.

Then his expression slid into a grin. "One more thing, Amber, you're correct about us not having the right bioelectrical whatever they're called. Fortunately, Sam rigged up an alternative."

He held it up in front of her, and she felt her mouth go slack with shock. It took her at least seven seconds until she could find her voice. "You're kidding me."

He shook his head. "Nope. Most sensitive biosensor we could find."

"And you put it in a *dildo?*"

23

"WHY WOULD YOU PUT a sensitive piece of equipment in a dildo? And think that you could get accurate readings?"

Roger pulled a serious face. She knew it was just a fake face though, because his eyes were dancing with suppressed laughter. "Sam said the same thing. He suggested we add nipple sensors, too—"

"You are kidding me—"

"But I said that was just overkill."

"Boys and their toys," she said. "You are insane. Certifiable. Absolut—" She gasped as he started to insert it inside her. It wasn't difficult. After all, he was still standing in the V of her legs and she was still cuffed to his desk. Plus, she'd been more than ready for something to go there for a little while now. But a dildo?

He tapped a key on his computer and the thing began to turn ice cold.

"Oh, my God!" she gasped as she tried to straighten off the desk.

"Oh, hell. Wrong key. Sorry." He hit another and the temperature shifted again, warming to a lovely soft heat. "Better?"

She didn't know how to answer. She couldn't believe that

she was sitting here like this. That he had…and she had al-lowed…and… It was vibrating. A low soft pulse of power that felt wonderful.

"Um…" she said, licking her lips.

Then he shifted, sliding his other hand back between her thighs. He pushed it deeper into her with steady, relentless pressure. She didn't think she'd be able to accommodate it all, but then his other fingers began their magic. He began to caress her, his thumb rolling up and over her clit.

Before long, she felt her body beginning to flex, her back arching, her legs tightening around his. He didn't move, but his fingers still did. Up and around her clit. A long circle. A slow push. God, he knew just what she liked. And when he bent his head to suckle on her nipple, she didn't care that she was spread-eagled on his desk. She just wanted more. Right then.

An electronic chime sounded, and Roger straightened. Her nipple turned cold from the wetness, but he didn't look like he was returning to it any time soon. Even his manipulations between her thighs stopped. He didn't pull his hand away, but he stopped moving as he looked at the screen.

"All set," he said calmly.

She blinked. She was anything but calm right then, and he knew it.

"Okay, look at the screen. See how the graph is bobbing right there in the happy green zone. That's for truth. For re-laxed and happy."

"But I'm not relaxed," she said. She was aroused. She was nearly orgasmic. She was definitely not relaxed.

"Right, right. I misstated. This is the preorgasmic state. I call that relaxed and happy. This, on the other hand, is the unhappy state."

He abandoned her to hit a key, and just like that, the dildo changed temperature. It went from warm and pulsing to still and freezing cold in two breaths.

"Oh!" she cried. "Oh, my God, stop it!"

The machine let out a heavy clunking sound.

"Unhappy," he said as he hit the key again. The cold eased off, but it didn't heat and it certainly didn't begin pulsing again.

"And this is neutral," he said. On the screen, the line indicator sat near the middle.

"And this is a lie detector how?"

"The computer has read the extremes of your state."

"Not the full extreme," she groused. After all, she hadn't orgasmed yet, and frustration was kicking in.

He grinned. "Well, not all, but close enough. So now we go back to our game."

"I am really getting tired of this game."

"Really?" he said, his expression teasing. "And here I thought you were starting to get into it."

She grimaced at him. "What's your question?"

He leaned forward, his lips almost to hers. She didn't move, didn't reach forward to kiss him because she didn't want to give in so easily. So she just stayed absolutely still while he asked his question.

"Do you believe that deep down, our core values are a lot closer than you thought?"

"You mean national health care or privatized? Capitol punishment or lifetime incarceration? Bert or Ernie?"

His eyes narrowed. He knew she was purposely being difficult.

"You have to make your questions specific for the results to have any validity."

He looked her over slowly, his gaze sliding from the top of her head down to her spread legs, then back up. "You're stretched out in the hottest position I've ever seen, and you have the nerve to question my questions?"

She lifted her chin, secretly thrilled that he thought she looked hot like this. Oddly enough, it was working for her, too. "The one has nothing to do with the other."

He grunted. "Tell that to my dick."

"Get your dick as close to me as your dildo and I will."

He snorted, but she felt the tremor in his hands. After all, they were pressed rather intimately against her.

"Very well," he said. "Specifically, do you believe that you and I are close enough in our core energetic versus scientific opinions that we can still have a loving and happy relationship?"

"Yes," she said honestly. Because, yes, hadn't they just established that not more than fifteen minutes ago?

Chime.

He smiled beatifically at her and they both looked at the monitor. The line was bobbing in the happy zone.

"Truth. Okay, next question."

"Nope. I answered truthfully. So you owe me a forfeit. Get your pants off now."

He blinked. Obviously, he'd forgotten their earlier game. But she could see he was willing. If the tent in his pants was any indication, he was beyond willing. A minute later, he stood before her in only his silk boxers, and the electronic indicator bobbed a little higher into the happy zone.

"Next question," he said. "Will you marry me?"

She stiffened, her mind screeching to a halt. This was not how a girl wanted to be proposed to. And it certainly wasn't what she'd expected while in the middle of their game.

Clunk.

Roger turned his head to the monitor as the line indicator dropped into the distinctly unhappy zone. "I'll take that as a no."

"Roger—"

He shook his head. "No, I understand. And for the record, when I really do propose, it's going to be a lot more romantic than this."

She sighed. "Roger—"

"I just wanted you to see how much you stiffen up when you're afraid."

"I'm not afraid!" she said hotly.

He jerked his chin toward the monitor. "The clunk disagrees with you. You are afraid. You are stiff and upset—"

"This is so not fair!" she cried as she purposely turned her head away from the computer. "Marriage is serious, Roger. It's not for discussion during sex games!"

"Not usually," he said softly. "But you're not a usual girl, are you? So answer this, Amber…"

His voice trailed away while she waited for the question. And when it didn't come, she turned back to face him. Apparently that was what he needed because he finally spoke.

"Do you love me?"

Oh, God, he looked like a lost puppy dog. There was so much uncertainty in his voice that her insides just melted. And one look at his face told her that he was very afraid of her answer. Silly man. She'd realized she was in love a while ago. She just hadn't wanted to say the words aloud, even in her own mind—but she did.

"Roger," she admonished softly, "do you honestly think I'd be in this position with a man I didn't love?"

Chime.

His eyes lit and his whole body jerked forward. She went for him as well, meaning to wrap her arms around him and do what she'd been aching to all evening. But she was still handcuffed, and her arms were pulled up short by the cold metal.

"Damn it, Roger. Get these things off me."

He shook his head. "Not yet. Not when it's working." As proof, he gestured to the computer where it did indeed read happy. Well, up until the dip when the cuffs jerked her movements short.

"You don't need a lie detector to know that I'm serious when I tell you I love you."

"Really?" he said, an honest question in his voice. "How long have you known? You haven't said anything before now. When did you first realize you loved me?"

She bit her lip. She didn't want to answer that one because he already knew the answer.

"Amber?"

Clunk.

"Amber? Please. The truth."

"In Arizona," she said quietly. "I started thinking the word back then."

"About the time you decided we didn't suit at a core level. About the same time you started thinking you had to break up with me. Am I right, Amber?"

She couldn't look at him. And she damn well wasn't going to look at the computer which was about to clunk in loud, obnoxious tones. And she couldn't respond. Not now. Not when he'd just ripped open a wall into her to reveal the truth.

It was true. She was afraid.

Chime.

She opened her eyes and spun to look at the monitor. It couldn't possibly be indicating that she was happy. She was as far from happy as she could get.

"What were you thinking just then, Amber?" Roger asked, his voice tight with emotion. "Whatever it was, it was true. This just indicates when you're relaxed enough to be honest."

Rather than speak, she shook her head, her eyes shutting tight with tears.

"Oh, shit, don't cry," he gasped. "Shit, I've done this all wrong."

She gasped in surprise as the dildo was removed. A moment later, he was fumbling at her wrists. One cuff, then the other, clicked open and her arms were free. Then his hands were on her face, his thumbs wiping away her tears as he pressed tiny kisses to her chin, her cheek and finally her lips.

"I'm sorry, I'm sorry," he kept saying between kisses. "I thought if I got you horny, I could get to the truth." He pulled back to look in her eyes. "You know, mix a little science with a sex toy, and *bam*, you're playing. You're relaxed. I thought I could get you to admit the truth. I'm so sorry."

She pressed her fingers to his lips, cutting off his words. She had to say the truth. He deserved to know.

"You're right, Roger. I am afraid. I don't know why. It's not like I've had some big relationship trauma."

His lips curved beneath her fingers, and he slowly lifted away. "Everyone's afraid, Amber. Relationships are hard. Commitment is ten times harder. It's just you geniuses who completely freak at the idea. I think it's because everything else is so obvious to you. Everything comes easy. Everything, that is, except for the one thing that's damn hard for everyone."

"Relationships?"

He shook his head. "Love, Amber. I love you. You love me. That's damn scary. I just can't have you running from it." He took a deep breath. "If you're taking the job at Mandolin because that's what you want, then fine. But don't go running to Arizona because you're afraid of what we have. Of what we could be."

He was right. God, he was so damn right, she couldn't believe she hadn't seen it before. Fear was natural. And when Amber was afraid, she usually ran. Into her work. Into another state. Into whatever she could find to bury herself away from the fear.

"I'm not going to run," she said quietly.

"Good."

"But…" She bit her lip.

"You're still afraid. I know. So am I. But we'll work it out. We'll get past it together. We're both too stubborn to allow anything else to happen."

She nodded. He *had* addressed everything she was thinking. God, it was freaky the way he read her mind like that. Of course, that was probably just his intuition kicking in.

"But there's something else. Something I haven't told you yet," she said.

He stroked his hand along her cheek, and she leaned into his caress. "Yes?" he prompted.

"Your doctor called me."

He froze. "My doctor? Why?"

"Well, he was very interested in what we'd done. Said he'd never seen such a dramatic shift in blood pressure before."

Roger frowned. "Yeah, he said stuff like that to me, too."

"Well, he was very interested. In everything I've been doing."

It took a moment for Roger to process what she was saying. Was it possible? "Are you saying there might be a job here for you? At a clinic that is open to your ideas?"

She nodded, happiness starting to well up inside her. "We're just talking right now, but yeah, it looks like there could be work for me here. It's not a great job compared to what's available at Mandolin. And the clinic certainly isn't any type of leader in medicine like Mandolin."

His face started to fall. "Amber, I know how much your job means to you. I know that you want to be at the cutting edge of medicine—"

"And I can be. Here in Chicago. Healing is about one

patient at a time. Your blood pressure. Mary's arthritis. I can do that right here. With you."

His mouth was open in surprise, which quickly shifted to wariness. "Amber, are you sure? I mean, Mandolin is a lot to give up."

She shook her head, growing more confident with the notion. "You're worth it. I just didn't see it before because I was too afraid." Then she grinned as she trailed her hands down his chest and to the top of his shorts. "Okay, psychic. Tell me what I'm thinking?"

"Uhh," he stammered. "I never said I was psychic."

"Oh, right. Intuition. Okay, I'll tell you. I answered the last question honestly."

His body had tightened, and his hands started sliding from her face, caressing downward over her shoulders. "Yes, you did."

"So you owe me an item of clothing."

"I've only got one left." His boxers.

"Roger," she whispered as she pushed down his shorts. "I've got a confession."

His hands paused right before they touched her breasts. "Yes?"

"I've always wanted a high-powered, intuitive executive to do me on his desk."

His eyebrows arched. "Really?"

"Oh, yeah."

"Well, I'm a high-powered executive." His hands finally slipped to her breasts, cupping and teasing them just how she liked.

She arched into his caress, letting her head fall back. "Yes, Roger. Yes, you are."

"And I believe," he said as his lips trailed down to her left nipple, "that I'm pretty intuitive, too."

She gasped as his lips latched on and began to suck. "Yes, I think you qualify. Oh!"

The fire was building beneath her skin. Her legs were going weak and she had to lean back against the desk again for support. He followed her forward, his tongue never faltering as he suckled.

She braced her elbows back, silently thankful that he'd had the foresight to clear it off. "Tell me you have condoms," she gasped.

"Around you?" he said as he switched to her other nipple. "Always."

She grabbed his face and hauled him up for a deep kiss. It lasted too long and not long enough. Then she pushed him away.

"Suit up!"

He grinned and did as he was told. Apparently, he'd bought a whole new box and it was right inside the drawer behind the handcuffs. And when he was done, he returned to her mouth, then her cheeks, then one ear.

"On your back? Or bent over the top?" he asked.

She wrapped her legs around him and pulled him tight. She was so ready. He filled her in that single move, and he was a zillion times better than any bioelectronic probe. He was Roger. And he loved her just as much as she loved him.

"Good choice," he gasped as he took hold of her hips. She helped him build to the right rhythm, tightening and releasing her legs in time with him.

"It's not an either-or," she answered, her words coming out in breathless gasps. "This is only phase one."

His eyes opened wide in surprise, but thankfully, his rhythm didn't falter. "I love you," he breathed.

"I love you," she answered.

Their tempo increased. He moved his hands beneath her

bottom, cupping her against the friction. She helped him, angling her pelvis in just the perfect way.

He thrust. She gripped.

Once more.

Yes!

Orgasm ripped through her, destroying the last of that wall of fear. He exploded as well, his spirit imbedding deep inside her body and her heart. She closed her eyes to savor the moment. Her orgasm was already fading, but there was an entire ocean of joy as she let her mind absorb what he'd just told her.

He loved her, and she loved him. Everything else would work out.

"Yes," she whispered before any doubts could creep in.

He blinked, lifting his forehead off her shoulder. "What?"

"Yes," she repeated. "Yes, I will marry you."

His face lit with joy. Even his body reacted, lifting with pleasure. "Yes?"

She smiled. "Are you doubting my answer? Can't your ultrasensitive bioprobe tell you whether I'm telling the truth or not?"

He grinned, then swooped in for a kiss. A deep one that expressed more clearly than words exactly what he thought and felt.

"I think," he said, "that we're going to have to test this particular lie detector over and over in the coming years."

"I can support that particular line of study."

He grinned. "Excellent." Then he waggled his eyebrows as his gaze flickered over his desk. "Now I believe you said something about phase two..."

Epilogue

CLAIRE CAME IN EARLY, as was her wont on Monday mornings. She liked getting everything set to rights before people came in. And she especially liked greeting them at their Monday-morning most vulnerable and finding out what they'd been doing over the weekend. It wasn't politically correct of her, but she loved knowing the people she worked with, especially their weekend habits and any piece of gossip she could glean. But first the coffee had to be started, the doors unlocked and the security tapes scanned.

It was a little detail, but one she took seriously. They were in a high-end technological business. It was important to know who was coming in on weekends to do what. It wasn't nearly as invasive as it sounded. The cameras were in the lab to record what happened in case of an accident, and in the hallways, too. But nothing in the offices unless you left your office door open. Then she could get a good view, usually of paperwork and computer screens.

She was sipping her morning latte when she saw it. Or rather them. Roger, apparently, had forgotten the camera outside his office. Or maybe he'd been too busy to think of shutting his office door. Either way, it was quite the show.

She fast-forwarded as quickly as she could, then deleted

that very long section of the recording. Just because she liked to know the office secrets didn't mean she had to share that information with anyone else. Then she reached over and picked up the phone to order a dozen vegan muffins from the bakery next door.

It was only after she hung up the phone that she sat back and thought about what she'd seen.

"Okay," she murmured. "So not gay."

* * * * *

COMING NEXT MONTH

Available March 29, 2011

#603 SECOND TIME LUCKY
Spring Break
Debbi Rawlins

#604 HIGHLY CHARGED!
Uniformly Hot!
Joanne Rock

#605 WHAT MIGHT HAVE BEEN
Kira Sinclair

#606 LONG SLOW BURN
Checking E-Males
Isabel Sharpe

#607 SHE WHO DARES, WINS
Candace Havens

#608 CAUGHT ON CAMERA
Meg Maguire

You can find more information on upcoming
Harlequin® titles, free excerpts and more at
www.HarlequinInsideRomance.com.

REQUEST YOUR FREE BOOKS!
2 FREE NOVELS PLUS 2 FREE GIFTS!

red-hot reads!

Selene wanted nothing to do with the father of her son, Alex; but Aristedes had other plans…that included them.

*Read on for an sneak peek from
THE SARANTOS SECRET BABY by Olivia Gates,
available April 2011, only from Harlequin Desire.*

"You were right to turn my marriage offer down," Aristedes said.

And Selene found her voice at last, found the words that would not betray the blow he'd dealt her. "Thanks for letting me know. You didn't have to come all the way here, though. You could have just let it go. I left yesterday with the understanding that this case is closed."

Before the hot needles behind her eyes could dissolve into an unforgivable display of stupidity and weakness, she began to close the door.

The door stopped against an immovable object. His flat palm.

"I can't accept that." His voice was low, leashed.

What did her tormentor mean now? Was he ending one game only to start another?

She raised eyes as bruised as her self-respect to his, found nothing there but solemnity and determination.

Before she could voice her confusion, he elaborated. "I never let anything go unless I'm certain it's unworkable. I realize I made you an unworkable offer, and that's why I'm withdrawing it. I'm here to offer something else. A workability study."

She leaned against the door, thankful for its support and partial shield. "Your son and I are not a business venture you can test for feasibility."

His gaze grew deeper, made her feel as if he was trying to delve into her mind, take control of it. "It's actually the